V J WAKS
RABBIT
HOLE

RabbitHole

Front Cover design by Paul Kime.
Cover layout and design by Scott Ross of Wave's End
Services, LLC., and Jeff Valent.

Printed in the United States of America.

This book is printed on acid-free paper.

This book is a work of fiction; people, places and
situations do not reflect historical events.

I wish to extend my heartfelt thanks to those whose contributions
made this work possible, including:

M.R.   E.P.
E.T.   J.P.
C.A.   B.B.
C.C.L.N.
And
She Who is Not To Be Named

Those who restrain their desire, do so because theirs is weak enough to be restrained.

WILLIAM BLAKE

RABBITHOLE

V. J. WAKS

Chapter 1

THE MOUNT

"I hate it here.

I'm sorry, Abby, but I do. Nothing connects me here – not anymore. There's just one place in the entire town that I don't hate. And everyone in there is dead."

The young man sprang up from his chair.

Anger fueled the rapid-fire strides that brought him to the library's high windows. Like a tethered beast, there Caspian Hythe stood and glared out onto the gardens as if at a mortal enemy. Then, as it had done repeatedly since his arrival here weeks ago, his gaze flew skyward. Once more, circling high above the Hythe house and the town – there was the bird of prey.

There he is – who can go when and where he pleases.

Here am I – who cannot.

The bird seemed aware of his thoughts. Its flight immediately canted; now it wheeled away hard, east, across the river, drawing his eyes after.

To Castle Hill.

Rays of late day sun pushed through the curtain's lace; they danced in bright turbulence across the face of Mrs. Hythe's only nephew. Deceptively calm, Abigail studied the young man at the window, seeing in her mind the father as well.

How very like Randolph, when he was just that age. It was a revelation simple and still too personal. After a year's worth of counting out the days, she had never told Cass how very much she still missed the late Randolph Hythe. She sat back in her chair, surrounded by the common threads that family and shared tragedy wear.

Sprawling, majestically high with its facing of hoary stone hung with ivy and moss, this house in Guildford had always been her brother's favourite.

How quickly it had become just as beloved to his new wife and bright- eyed little boy, a little boy who here had spent his very first English Christmas. He had grown with every visit, marveling each Yuletide as frost had worked a subtle magic on the windows, as the season had opened a deeper sorcery in the expansive gardens that stretched around the house. Sharp eyed and questing, Caspian Hythe had listened, rapt, as carolers in the streets brought the old songs right to their doors.

The season was turning; the carolers would come again soon. Guildford was a modern, industrial town. But, the old ways were still cherished here and as another winter neared, the past tugged at Abby's heart – Yuletide, the old ways, the old legends.

At the same windows that had lent such fascination before, the boy that had been stood now as a young man; empty of peace, bitter, hating the place.

The place he despised was nonetheless remarkable. The town's lazy river still wended in cool greenness along its towpath. A profitable market town since the Middle Ages, Guildford had steadily grown about the Wye's golden sands, adding tidy houses and tourism. Abigail Hythe's love for the town and the family house had never faltered. That family had diminished suddenly, without warning, as death had claimed first Cass' mother and then all too soon – his father.

One of the last, oldest Victorian mansions on the Guilddown Road, this house remained a marvel. East, its terraced gardens faced the river. But it was at its northern boundary that the house whetted true fascination, sweeping up high to touch the very feet of Guildford's famous cemetery – the wind- swept burial ground of the Mount.

And everyone there is dead….

For those with a very particular kind of leaning, the vista to the east might have held a deeper fascination. If one stood in the Hythe garden and looked across the Wye, one would actually see it – there on the eastern shore, on its own high hill– the Castle. Old before the coming of the Saxons, the Castle's ancient pile had awakened something in her brother's only child. It had been Cass himself who, pointing wildly with a then pudgy digit, had named the place.

'Gasties, Papa. Gasties!' he had cried, dragging his father after him. It was as close as a very young, very bright boy could get to a very old word; his own childish rendering for *'gaistaz'* – the archaic word for 'ghost'.

Ghost.

A strange word to teach a child – perhaps the father thought the child would forget it.

The child did not forget it.

The boy soon made regular beelines for the gate that led under the trees and out of the garden where one of the many footbridges would take him over the Wye – from there, into the Castle's ruins, where he would lose himself for hours, hidden under the tree's shadows, summer after summer.

Until last year; when the visits abruptly ceased.

"You never used to hate it here," she reminded him. "You are connected to me. And you are connected to this place, in ways you can't imagine – as was your father and his father as well."

Cass tore his eyes from the sky, from the vistas of wet, grey trees, their leaves scattering explosively in a brisk, early autumn wind. His fingers ran through hair as full and black as had been his father's. When he looked back at her, confusion and pain filled the bright blue eyes that had been sharp with anger moments ago.

"I'm .. I have to go out, Abby," he said. She nodded.

"It gets dark so early now, Cass, do be careful. We're still having a bit of nastiness around here."

"The 'mad dog' thing again?"

Her grey eyes darkened with a look that made him pause, but she went on.

"It must be a dog – mustn't it?"

"This makes it – ten – doesn't it?" Cass wondered.

"It does indeed. This time it was a cat – but closer this time, Cass, very close, just across the lane. They found it in pieces this morning. It has to be the work of someone's pet, gone monstrously wrong."

Someone's pet – gone monstrously wrong.
Monstrously wrong.

He saw in his own mind the bloody events of the day before. He'd been right there when it had happened, right before his eyes – in the village main street, where a man had viciously attacked and tried to kill his neighbor's dog – a hound – because he thought the animal savage enough to be the killer that, in panicked desperation – all were seeking.

Who are the monsters here?

"I'll keep my eyes open," Cass said.

He took up his jacket and moved to the library doors that led out onto the grounds. With his long fingers poised over the ornate metal knob, Cass looked back at his aunt again; then he was gone.

When she rose, Abby's face and demeanor had lost all vestiges of calm.

She, too, stopped before the windows. For the space of several long moments, she looked out, marking her nephew's progress as he walked quickly across the lawns.

Beside the windows on her desk, the morning paper lay open. Its headlines blaring, inescapable; its front page was a lurid mockery, bloated with the grisly details of yet one more slaughter.

'Another Surrey Puma? Has the Mystery Beast from the '60's Returned to Kill Again?'

Reaching across the desk, she opened its drawer and took out once more the small journal.

Brown and stained, with its worn leather cover and yellowed pages, the journal stayed in her hand.

Abigail Hythe was no longer in doubt.

Her nephew was not there to see. Had he been, it would not have been the look of dread flashing momentarily across her face that would have caused him uncertainty – and alarm.

It would have been the look on her face now – one of cold, merciless, implacable resolve.

T

You are the world's consummate ass.
That woman treats you like gold.
You've been here a fortnight.
Who haven't you managed to piss off?
You need to grow up.

He crossed the wide lawns, then bent low, passing under curling tree limbs. The old gate's rusty hinges moaned sadly as he went through.

From here, one could go many ways: down, into the Town – or up.

Somehow before he'd set foot out of the house, his way seemed chosen. He drove himself to run up the rough path that coursed higher and higher. When he looked up, he found the hawk over him again, high, circling, its scream distant but strident, a spectral censure tearing across the sky. Stung, culpable – he redoubled his pace, reaching the tangled hillside at the top, where the land ended, merging precipitously into grey, open sky – at the Mount.

This is what I need.

What I need....

Catching his breath, he filled his lungs with damp, cold air, caught up by near silence. Here, as if in fealty to the place, the sounds of birds, the rustling of leaves in the breeze, all seemed muted. Thin fog began to drift among the monuments as he made his way across the hill, deeper into Guildford's oldest cemetery. The mist was a chill, wet soothing blanket, in perfect keeping with a place laden with antiquity and unplumbed mystery. The air grew colder; tendrils of white swirled down as he picked his way past the mossy head stones, somber requiems to a vastly different age.

A better age. Far better than this one.

As he walked here, toward the border where tall trees still remained, his thoughts were not on the tombs about him, but elsewhere.

He stopped finally at the very top of the Mount. Then, as he had done countless times before, all of his life – he looked east. The tops of the Castle's broken stone walls, skeletal and grey, reached skyward like fingers pushing up from a forgotten grave. The ruins caught the sun's last rays as true dusk began to fall.

The ruins looked down upon the town; under that mindful gaze, time turned backward. Once, lush, deep woods had reigned there; the trees had not surrendered easily to the insistent centuries. Scattered across the site, proud bits of forest held calm, imperious sway. Plaintive and demanding in his mind were the memories of his visits. For, rising from the relic's earth under the trees had come to a young, very willing mind the faded essence of unremembered years, the strange, rich aroma of loam and deep, unquiet earth.

The ancient Lords walked upon that same earth.

Before the horse drawn carriages, the buses, the hollow noise of this misbegotten, modern age – long, long ago – there was majesty.

There was wonder.

It lay there still, like the perfume of blooms long dead, the lingering scent of petals pressed in an old book. The sunlight failed to penetrate the shade below those remaining trees, retreating instead before the sentinels of the past.

A past replete with death – just like mine.

United by bonds forged in time and blood – they faced each other, the Castle and the Mount. The young man was still, yet not at peace – he breathed in air that was bitter and keen with loss, his vision dimmed by the past and his own tears. In his mind were the words he could not have told to Abby, words she must have known, that haunted him still.

That last summer.

We never made it back there, did we, Dad?

I couldn't save you.

I can't save anyone, I can't even save myself.

Long lines of graves were at his back.

One of them belonged to Randolph Hythe.

It was a grave still new, still fresh after a year's rough, climactic passage – waiting for homage, for pardon that had not yet come. The dead man's only son tried to turn away from it, to put it from his mind, but the mood of the place claimed him. He saw, yet did not see that the sun had begun to sink below the lip of encroaching cloud.

Surrounded by death and the dead and the dark memories that the place had stirred, Cass was suddenly spent.

Why had he come here? Here, to claim him, was every memory, every phantom….

There's nothing left for me to lose.

The wind rose suddenly. Like a physical blow, it struck him full in the face.

With it, from the midst of turmoil, a strange penetrating calm suddenly descended, miraculously taking hold, for from outside him the thread of other thoughts was rising, in a voice not his own, distant yet not unfamiliar.

There is no escape from what we have known and been.

Do not seek escape. Here in this place is what you seek, what will bridge past and future, what will unite what you have been with what you will become.

Find it. Then return. Return and begin.
Compass the task that must be done.
It is at hand.
What dost thou desire?

He was stunned – mystified and confused by his need to listen, to heed what could only be imagination. But, cold and blinding, clutching at him like so many icy fingers, fog was now everywhere. He pulled away from its grip; he had to find his way down, now, while he could still do so.

It was then that the first sound reached him.
My God, what was that?

It was the cry of an animal; only a cry. But it was shocking – short, piercing, nothing less than a fatal cry, terrible in its final, throbbing brevity.

Mist curled about him but torn between the need to get off the Mount while he could yet see – and an unexpectedly overpowering need to know – Cass froze in his tracks. Reason calmed him. It had to be the work of a fox. Foxes still came here; a fox must have killed something. Here was prey. The occasional badger and innumerable cats roamed freely through the cemetery's grounds, unhindered, virtually untouched by the nearby press of noisy, modern humanity.

There was nothing to hear now but the thin voice of the wind in the grasses. Still he stood, unmoving, listening – waiting.

Then it came – floating in the air, at first from everywhere at once, then from one direction alone – more frightful than the death cry of any animal.

Horrifying, an echo that fell slowly away – this was what galvanised him to run – not away from that last uncanny resonance – but towards it.

It was like nothing he had ever heard in his life – a warble, low, rasping yet melodious. Snarling, musical, utterly unnatural, it had come from a thick stand of bushes ahead. Cass moved closer to them. His steps slowed and he stopped again, mere paces away from the small grove, his mind racing.

Are you crazy? What are you doing?

Well, you're here and whatever it was, it must be gone by now.

You hope.

He picked his way forward until he stood directly before the thicket. There, he knelt and slowly parted the stems and twigs with his bare hands.

A fox had not been the perpetrator.

It had been the victim.

The body was still warm. Steam rose from the crumpled form under the bush. Blood was everywhere; the fox's throat had been torn open. The split breastbone showed white and jagged, and blood streaked the snowy breast fur. Rich and red, more blood lay smeared over forelimbs that still twitched spasmodically.

What did this?

So quickly – in broad daylight?

Where did it go?

Even in the gloom, he had seen nothing leave the thicket. A light rain pattered down but Cass studied the ground, painstakingly working over the area around the fox. Finally he stopped. Stunned and fearful, he sat back on his heels.

Caspian Hythe looked about him – suddenly needing to be sure, very sure, that whatever had just been here and had just done this – was truly gone.

For it had left other evidence of its eagerness to kill, if not to eat.

There in the damp soil, he had found the tracks of what had killed the fox.

They coursed across the wet ground, blood-stained, splayed, each greater than the length of his fingers – they were the indents of horrific digits.

It was clear that those digits were tipped with claws.

Deep enough to see in the failing light, the prints resembled those of no animal he knew.

Like nothing I have ever seen before.

Chapter 2

A TRIP IN THE DARK

Abby's tea was interrupted by the slamming of the door that led from the library out onto the gardens.

She reached the windows too late -- all she saw of Cass was a flash of his jacket and backpack as he ran down the terraced brick walks and sprinted across the lawn, vanishing through the gate that led to the Mount.

Abby went out and stood on the stone terrace. It was her own terrace and her own gardens that lay before her, but Abby was trembling – her eyes searched the shadows of the high hedge whose thick foliage encircled the grounds.

Her eyes stayed on the hedge as she backed slowly to the door.

Then she turned and quickly entered the house. She went immediately to the desk, drawing out her Tarot deck, placing the uncut deck before her. Then she sat back in her chair, breathing deeply, composing herself – to wait.

By now, with torch in hand, her nephew had regained the blood-drenched thicket on the Mount. The light was nearly gone, moisture was settling over the grounds but it didn't stop him. Starting at the mangled and stiffening body of the fox, his search soon covered a fair amount of the cemetery.

It was fruitless; there was no sign of the killer. What he had found by the torn, bloody remains remained unique – and uniquely unidentifiable.

Dog? Cat? What? What else could it be?
What the Hell else lives up here – badgers?
Bats? Zombies?
What?

Night slowly descended upon the Mount. A pensive young man returned to the house. There, an utterly preoccupied young man finished dinner and sipped a glass of port with the aunt who regarded him with concern, but without question.

Late night found him upstairs in his rooms, with his wineglass at his laptop. Cass was proud of his game programming skills; tonight would normally be perfect for playing with those games.

It was not to be a normal night.

Instead, he was combing the web for data on animal spoors. To no avail; the tracks were clear in his mind; their likeness appeared nowhere. Long searching left him nonplussed; he finally halted from sheer exhaustion.

It was very late and the house was utterly quiet.

Truly tired now, it was with aching fingers that he rubbed his brow. He tossed down the next to last dregs of wine, then tapped out the final few moves of an habitual game of solitaire. The next card would be the Queen of Hearts; he placed the cursor on her card.

But his eyelids fluttered; he no longer knew what to make of the day. The cry of an owl from somewhere in the trees outside helped him shake off sleep.

In the next instant, he was shaking his head again – but now he was wide awake, completely awake – and staring at the computer screen.

He was staring at the Queen of Hearts – whose florid red emblems seemed different somehow; he looked again.

What the Hell.

Before his eyes, the face of the Queen on the card was no longer as it should be. It was growing larger and larger, until it nearly filled the screen.

The rich red of her symbols was changing. Moment by moment, darkness crept across the card's face until, in three amazed breaths – every heart on her card was black, inky black. Like peep-holes that opened into a shuttered room, the darkness of the Queen's hearts beckoned – and Cass gazed into them as if they might be doorways in fact.

His room was markedly still. It was a silence so deep, so profound, that it seemed an actual presence. All around him was a curious absence of sound, one that was palpable, gripping and icy with threat.

His breath caught in his throat. Out of the darkness of the heart that the Queen herself held – a deeper midnight seemed to well up. And from inside that shadowed place, gradually growing into shape and substance – he saw the form of a girl.

A young woman, rather. Aware, yet unaware that he must be dreaming, that he had to be dreaming, it couldn't be anything else – he nonetheless saw her. In faded jeans and loose sweater, she lay stretched across a sofa. The soft glow from the ornate lamp on the table close by her head lit both her and the room. She was fair, with bright red hair that played about her face as she frowned and moved in her sleep, for asleep she certainly seemed to be.

In the hand that was nearest to him – she held something.

It was a card, a single playing card.

Cass leaned closer. The sleeper roused and turned, exposing the card face to his view.

It's the Queen of Hearts.

Like the card in his game – her card's hearts were also black.

They were as black as the eyes of the Queen whose face came alive on his screen, whose ebony eyes moved, searching – exactly as living eyes would move. They looked out from the beautiful ivory face, finding and intently returning the gaze of the young man, who sat utterly baffled, utterly at sea with what he now saw, in a suddenly frigid room.

The low, horrid laughter he heard came from the face on his screen and a voice, harsh and resonant and taunting rang in his ears.

The grandfather wouldn't.
The father – he couldn't.
See the Name writ in stone
And the Child he once knew!
Seeds not meant for sowing,
Tears hidden, not showing,
Only together – they tell what to do!
Will the son do the seeking?
The fighting – the wreaking?
Far too great is the task –
For one such as you!

The darkness of the Queen's eyes changed again – from deep within the black orbs, shadowy forms beckoned, daring him to look deeper.

Suddenly Cass recoiled in horror – frantically he tried to pull away, to put distance between himself and the thing that was quickly filling his mind.

The screen had gone utterly dark.

Out of that darkness, shadows had stirred to life. Slowly, from the heart of the blackness – teeth – long, and sharp and brilliant white, appeared, and the red that should have made up the Queen's hearts and robes now glowed out of that darkness as dazzling red eyes. It was like a physical shock – he sensed rather than saw that the girl on the couch cried out, he knew with certainty that her hands had clutched upward — in terror.

From deep within the horrific image on the screen, a savage, bestial snarl erupted.

The room spun around him. With walls and ceiling tilting madly sideways – he found himself on the floor on his hands and knees, the echo of soft laughter fading in his ears.

Chilled, shaking, with sweat dampened hair, Cass forced himself to his feet, reaching for the wine glass. It was where he had left it. But, the last drops of wine were there no longer – a stream of mist, pale, icy and opaque, hung impossibly in the air above the now empty glass.

On the laptop, gone was the mocking face, gone the monstrous visions. The screen was once more just a screen, the game of solitaire just a game and precisely as they should have been, the game cards lay spread across bland green wallpaper.

The Queen of Heart's card was no different; her hearts were red, her face mild and placid, flat and unremarkable.

Cass stumbled away from the desk to the windows where, across the gardens below, a true autumn night stretched. Flinging open the casements, he breathed deeply, as might one who had just escaped a drowning pool. He was once more in control. He had failed, however, to convince himself that what had just occurred had not. But the air was bracing; he looked out once more.

Lustrous in the night, with its trees and groomed paths, the garden lay vividly illumined. Beyond, across the garden and up the hill, he caught a glimpse of the Mount's dark lanes, stark with moonlight.

A sudden chill reclaimed him.

Good God. What now?

It was up at the Mount, just visible at the nearest edge of the cemetery's somber grounds.

Moving against the wind, it pulsed, and hovered and played as though alive.

It was not a figure there, nor a reflection of something inanimate that had somehow caught and held the moonlight.

What he clearly saw there among the shadows of the monuments was small, dim, but indisputable – a very real circle of moving light.

ᛏ

Only inches high, it was enough to bring him to his knees.

Protruding from the wet turf, an edge of chipped headstone had caught the toe of his shoe just at the tip. Now he sat cursing, pulling wet leaves off his jacket, again wondering what exactly he thought he was doing out here.

The Mount.
Dead of night.
Alone.
Again.

His second race across the gardens and third visit that day to the Mount had disturbed only an owl. Ethereal yet massive, the creature had passed overhead, its wings eerily eclipsing the silhouettes of bats that reeled in the bird's soundless wake.

He, however, was still on the ground.

Cass was suddenly, deeply aware of the night. He was the stranger here; his was the shadow that did not fit, either in time or in place.

Get up, idiot.

He rose. Its outlines blurred by the low mist that eternally cloaked these grounds, the circle of light still floated elusively in the distance, at grave height. Bright enough to read by, the moon cast a stark light over what by day had appeared simply lonely, forlorn with barely hallowed antiquity.

It was a far different spectacle now.

Very slowly, he made his way amongst high stones whose carved angels sported the blemishes of a century and more of harsh winters and blazing sun. But his caution made it impossible to keep his eyes on both the light and the way.

When he looked again, the glimmer had vanished. There was no sign of life or anything else in the place, hard as he might look; there was nothing to see.

The dead were here in abundance; they slept without a night light.

Irked, cold, he found his way back to the path, marking the time before starting down.

What had been here tonight might well be here again.

Chapter 3

CARDS

I'll sleep when I'm dead.

Just before dawn, his pillows went onto the floor.

It's about cards; just some kind of game, that's all.

Why else the Queen of Hearts?

It's just about a game.

The early hours sped by with Cass locked to his laptop. A search for a better pencil led him around the room, and finally back to the desk where, crouching, he yanked at a stuck drawer. A hard pull freed the drawer and left him backwards on the floor with a pencil – and two decks of cards.

The first pack was a standard pack. There was the Queen of Hearts; her card, the colours, its form, and most importantly – the face of the Queen herself – all were unexceptional. What had leered out at him last night was like and yet very unlike what he now held in his hand.

The second deck was robed in black silk; it felt curiously heavy as he peeled off layer after layer of sheer cloth, until the cards lay bare on his palm.

A Tarot deck.

It's just a Tarot deck.

But it's so quiet now.

He halted in confusion; from the moment his naked hands had touched the cards, the room had gone dead still. Again, all about him was silence, one surreal, unnatural, disturbing, as though the room itself were listening to him, as if he were miles away from an old, creaky house and a garden burgeoning with restless life.

It's like I'm miles away.

Startled, he sat upright in the chair – for, harsh and insistent, a reply had come into his mind once again.

No, Caspian – not miles away.

Centuries away.

The hairs lifted on his neck in fear, in premonition – feelings so eerie, so strong that he couldn't imagine putting the deck down.

I need Abby now – Abby is precisely the one I need.

No wonder why – his aunt had read the cards since her own childhood – she had read them for him, all his own. Once he had asked her about them, the cards that had figured in the creation of every modern playing deck in existence. How it was that a person as educated, as worldly, as wise as was she, did not believe in free will?

'An excellent question,' she had replied. 'You exercised free will in asking it. And perhaps you were also *destined* to do so.'

He had smiled then; he was not smiling now.

For as he held the deck, his fingers and hands began to tingle. The sensation was becoming more and more pronounced as, one by one, he laid out all the major suit cards,

Again, overwhelmingly, inescapably came the wave of premonition, a sense of profound connection.

> *Last night – today – tomorrow.*
> *The link lies in your hand.*
> *Look at the cards.*
> *Look at them.*
> *The High Priestess. The Emperor.*
> *The Sorcerer – The Magus.*

The Magus.

Slowly, he collected the cards. His fist closed on the deck; he left the room. As he hurried down the hall with the deck still in his fist, he knocked once at the closed door of the room so near to his own. It was habitual; the room was inviolate, its door locked, its key lost. Abby had laughed when he had asked her about this room with its lost key, for she was one who was so well organized, one who never lost anything. 'Lost it is, probably lost it will remain until my last breath! Seriously – it will show up, Cass, I feel certain – for nothing is ever really lost, even when the last breath is.'

In the den, Abby looked up from her book to see Cass standing in the doorway. She smiled.

"Abby. I need you to do me a reading."

The smile on her face melted away.

Ŧ

Cass stood at the library windows. He stared out at the night; in silence, Abby stood in the doorway, waiting, watching, as emotion after emotion passed across her nephew's face.

Just hours ago Abby had laid out the cards for her nephew yet an extraordinary day was not yet over.

For she hadn't just read them for him. Instead, as if she had been waiting for precisely this moment, she had presented them to him as something quite different than what he had expected. How, long ago, a gift had come to guide the wise, to cleanse and fortify the hearts and minds of those fortunate – and courageous enough – to truly see.

Much, much later, Cass would come to wonder at this for, with that beginning, she would answer every unspoken question he had had. Suddenly a veil had been lifted from his eyes. It wasn't just Abby – still lovely, with her dark hair and her eyes so like his father's – whom he would come to see clearly in one golden afternoon, it was himself.

Gone was the senseless anger; gone, so much of the doubt. Now he told her what he had told no one – how his life had changed irrevocably, how much he had lost. His aunt had listened until there seemed no more words that he could say, not about pain, or fear.

"Or guilt, Cass."

The woman across from him on the den sofa had spoken very softly.

"You are not alone in this," she had said. "Could I have prevented it? Could I somehow have saved him – *could I somehow have seen?* You are not guilty merely because you are the one who has been left behind. Not even the mighty can see all ways; no one is infallible. But you must look to the path ahead and answer the need – to follow it. Truth is never easy to see, Cass. Reality – that is even harder to make out. You must use your eyes, use your head – but ultimately, you must trust your intuition. Whatever happens, whatever is going to happen – I promise you – I shall *always* be there for you, Caspian. *Always ready – at need.* Never forget this."

So that afternoon had passed away, with the young man and the woman sitting side by side, and her words would stay long in his memory. When the reading had finished, Abby had again poured wine for them and Cass swirled his in his glass.

Now, her eyes remained fixed upon him as he left the window, passed her, and moved to the stairs. He turned to her before starting up.

"I've got some work to do now," he said. "I'll be going out tonight – it will be very late. *But not too late – I hope.* I will be back."

She said nothing, but her eyes brightened.

"I know you will."

He went up the stairs.

Abby watched him go. She took up her own glass, and returned to the den, where, just hours before – blinding, unmistakable, and utterly unforeseen – affirmation had been given not only to Cass – but to her as well.

She had said nothing to him of what the cards had revealed to her then, nor what was in her heart now.

Abby returned to the table where the Tarot deck still lay, guarded by black silk. She lit a candle on the table top, then un-wrapped the deck once more. The cards felt familiar and soothing in her hands and she shuffled them, spreading them face down, in a wide arc. From the line, she chose one card. She turned it face up, placing it full in the candle's light, a light that rendered the ancient symbols startlingly clear.

Abby's face was emotionless as she studied the card – the regal figure there, the lions signifying bestial control, the black cat of dominion, a dominion rooted in darkness.

The Queen of Wands – Reversed.

The Queen of Hearts.

From the surface of the card – a pale mist, icy and opaque began to rise.

The room grew colder, darker. It was no longer a room, but a prison, a chamber where torture reveled, where minds and souls writhed helplessly, bound in thick darkness. One by one, shadows came to life, creeping forward like so many claws, claws that moved, seeking, reaching with a hunger undying and insatiable. They reached toward Abby, towards the candle whose flame had now begun to flicker, as if it struggled against a draft, potent yet unseen.

Abby's face was still emotionless.

She drew another card from the arc and turned it face upward – with its pillars, black and white, its full moon surmounting the regal head of the young Priestess, its solar cross denoting the balance of good and evil – the link between seen and unseen, full in latent power.

The High Priestess – against the Queen of Hearts.

With that thought, the mist blenched and shriveled. As it shred, the shadows drew back and once more the room was just a room, the candle burning with a flame once more brilliant and unfazed.

Slowly, Abby collected the cards. Then she placed them, swathed again in black silk, in the table's drawer.

When her hand returned back into the light, it was not empty.

She opened the velvet bag she held and reached within – the tiger wood wand, polished and gleaming, with its ebony tip and circlet of silver runes, lay in her hand.

She touched the wand; her fingers ran along the smooth wood. She turned it in the candle light, light that had suddenly grown stronger, brighter, suddenly more substantial, and she heard the front door open – then close softly.

She sat back in the chair. The wand remained before her, arrayed upon the dark wood of the table that had been her father's.

And his father's before him.

It is begun.

Chapter 4

FIRST, LIGHT

Bright over Guildford hung the full moon; brightly it shone on the Mount.

There, the clear air rang with the calls of night birds and the barely sensed trills of the bats as they wheeled over Cass.

Concealed by the tall shrubs and trees that ringed the southern edge of the graveyard, he waited. A restless wind played across the grasses. Above him, the moon circled as the slow hours crept by.

There.

Near the Mount's border closest to the river – a glimmer of light in the pale mist moved from headstone to headstone, weaving around the graves. Finally, it passed right before him then, still cloaked in mist, it started further up the hill.

No magic here.

Just a flashlight, like mine.

He untangled his cramped legs; he followed. It didn't take long.

Everything came to a halt in a natural culvert, where tall trees nearly eclipsed the moon. He drew closer. The massive down-swept arms of a stone angel curved over him as he crouched, hidden – and watched.

Not thirty paces away was a simple monument. Its flat ivory marker was surmounted by a high, white cross and there, the one that had carried the light now stood.

That light was now extinguished.

There was no longer any need for it. The flashlight hung limp in the watcher's hand as both he and the visitor by the grave stared, rapt and amazed.

There were more than two visitors to this grave that night.

For light there still was. A pulsing, soft aura of radiance danced impossibly in the space before the tomb.

At the very heart of the light, unnatural and spectral, there stood clearly another figure. Small it was, and thin, but it stood in plain sight, just as if it were day – as if it were alive.

It's a child. It's a little girl.

She wore a white dress, thin and clinging. Her arms and legs were bare in the night's chill, a chill that was penetrating, pervasive, one emanating from the figure itself. And without warning, the child that could not be a child, not in this place nor in this time, finished its own regard of the tomb and the white cross rising above it.

It turned. It stared directly back at the motionless watcher standing mere steps away, and Cass, hidden, transfixed, could see for himself the face of the thing that waited at the grave. Lovely and pale, with straight, smooth dark hair, the small face turned again. A wave of vertigo flooded through Cass for, this time – the dark, unseeing eyes, like bottomless black pools – stared directly into his own.

The child's pale hands shone with light. One of them rose to the white skin of her chest just above her dress – and the fingernails that passed across that skin came away dark with blood. The spirit knelt down. Its fingers dabbed back and forth over and across the cold, flat stone before the monument, in a grim parody of a quill being charged with ink. Again, and again, the nails went back and forth, from cold marble to colder flesh.

Close, too close, was the owl that passed overhead and Cass flinched, clutching at the short grass to steady himself.

When his eyes flew back to the grave, the unearthly glowing form was gone – and with its torch slipping from senseless fingers, the watcher at the tomb stumbled forward and fell to the ground.

He leapt up. He reached the figure; his hands went to the tumbled mass of limbs, shoes, coat and small bag. He was relieved beyond words that what he felt beneath his fingers seemed made of flesh and blood.

He pushed aside the jacket's hood to expose the watcher's face.

It's her. It's the girl I saw, it's her.

He raised her off the ground, spilling her red hair over his shoulder. The young woman roused, clutching at him with white fingers and her eyes and face were wild with fear.

That fear quickly changed to desperate relief, then doubt. The girl lay in his arms, her eyes searching his face, her voice low and plaintive.

"Did you see her? Did you see her, too?"

He nodded. He hauled her up onto her feet, then followed her to the grave itself.

On the flat white marble plate at the foot of the monument were lines of blood – words, written in blood dark with age, dried and black as blood could only be after long years had slipped away. A pale cold mist, unnatural and moving as if alive hung over the letters that even now were beginning to fade, lifting away in an icy spume. But before they did, before they vanished utterly from the cold white slab, both he and the girl read the words that had been scrawled there by a hand that no longer existed, had not existed as human for more than three quarters of a century.

Find the Servant, turn the Key.
Soul and Sorrow – set us free.

Cass studied the grave with its tall monument, with its simple white cross and its name writ there – the grave of Lewis Carroll – that had somehow drawn this apparition. On the frigid flat stone, now cleansed of its infernal message, the moon shone on the inscription that living men had carved into the bleak, white face.

"Where I am, there shall thy Servant be also."

T

"Drink it. Drink all of it. Don't move until you do."

He replaced the brandy in the high cabinet. Seated on the den sofa was the young woman with hair like flame. Her hands were steady. With sudden resolve, she set down her glass and looked at him.

"Say it again," she demanded.

"I saw her too."

"What did you see? What exactly did you see?"

He made a restless circuit of the room, struggling to force into some kind of accord what he had seen, with its insufficiency to natural law.

"What I saw was a child; the figure of a girl. Ten, maybe – in white, something pale, short, some kind of dress that hung close to her body."

"Like petals across her," she offered.

"Yes."

Somewhere between grey and green, his guest's eyes brightened.

"Her face?" she prompted.

"Pale – but her eyes…" The memory of those eyes, moving but black and empty of life came again and he swallowed hard. "Her eyes were dark, like her hair. Her hair was short and straight."

From outside, somewhere in the woods, there floated up the muted, cry of an animal – in pain.

There were woods out there and the sound came from far off. It was just a cry coming from out of the night. Yet both of them flinched, together they stared at the dark window; Cass broke the breathless silence.

"Maybe more work of 'The Surrey Puma.'"

That drew a look from his guest.

"The Surrey Puma," he continued. "What the papers suggest has been killing animals; again. First accounts started in the sixties; folks claim to have seen a cat-like thing hunting around the village. Same as then; things died."

She stared at the window again, as though she might see something there. She shook her head. Her voice was low in the room.

"It's not the Surrey Puma. It's not a puma at all."

He stared at her. "How do you know that?"

"It's not what they think. It's not what *you* think. *It's nothing you have ever seen before.*"

His jaw dropped. To hear her say that, his very thoughts – but coming from a stranger, from someone he had just met, and under such horrific circumstances – in his own mind, he was immediately back up at the Mount in an icy wind, standing over the body of a viciously mangled fox.

"What's your name," he asked, wishing his voice were steadier.

"Ava. Ava Fitzalan."

"Caspian Hythe. My friends call me Cass. Ava Fitzalan, there's something you need to see."

Chapter 5

PAIR OF HEARTS

"I'd say I don't believe it. Except that it's there."

Ava rose, then paced across his bedroom. She quickly returned to the desk and he let her take his place at the laptop.

Her fingers traced the line, the same course his own hand had traced when he'd laid out the grid, mapping the sequence of the attacks, each event, date by date. Their direction seemed as clear to her as it had been to him, and one by one, she followed them back, ending at their most likely origin – at the ruins across the river – Castle Hill.

"Damn," she said.

"Why 'damn'? Why there, Ava?" he demanded.

There was no reply.

He studied the map, then her. "It was you last night – up at the Mount – at the grave? Wasn't it?"

"Were *you* there then, too? *God.* Yeah, it was me. I needed to see her one more time, I needed some assurance I wasn't going crackers. Cass – did you recognise her? The little girl?"

He shook his head.

"I did. Tell me, what do you know about Alice Hargreaves – her more infamous name was Alice Liddell."

The moon that had paused behind clouds emerged suddenly. His rooms were flooded with light, a light as bright, as intangible as what had hovered about the specter at the grave. Ava's face and hair were transfigured; for a moment, he couldn't take his eyes off her.

She's so strong. So focused, so ready.
Ready for what?

She missed his cool appraisal, as well as the light of something new and warmer in his eyes. Intent on the screen, her lightning fast typing brought up a page with a photograph – old, beautiful, magical.

There, grainy with age and the technology of more than a century past, stood a young girl. Pale, with dark eyes and hair, her short dress clung, petal-like to her small form. Flanked on either side by leaves and foliage, her dark gaze was resolutely fixed on the camera and the one who held it – she seemed ethereal, fantastic, young and old, and otherworldly, all at once.

There on the screen was the image of the thing that had stood before the grave.

"He took her picture, Cass. He took lots of them. His were not the only ones, just the most notorious, I'd say."

"*He* did?"

"Of course he did. But what's this?" she asked.

Ava was frowning. Her finger hung over the image, over the leaves beside the girl's head just to the side of her face. It was just a patch of foliage; there was nothing to see but leaves, dappled in light and shadow.

"What are you talking about – what do you see?"

She stared at the image. "Something I've never seen before, something there – in the leaves."

He looked again; very carefully now, he regarded the tangled vegetation beside the young face, the leaves that framed her, almost cradling her in their voluptuous richness. Ava's frown deepened.

"Really? Cass, don't you see *anything* there –
right there, in the leaves?"

"No. Not yet, at least. Let's try something," he
replied.

He had a program that would clear this
image; in moments he had it open and uploaded the
photograph of the girl, leaves and all. With each pass
the image cleared, line by line, sharpening pixel by
pixel. As the ancient artefacts of dust and grime and
simple age fell away one after another, the image
grew more detailed. Finally, with the completion of
the last pass, the two sat mute.

The girl in the photograph was lovely, fragile,
fascinating, a dream-child all too real.

She was not alone.

There beside the girl's pale, lovely form,
another face was faintly but undeniably visible in
the leaves. With eyes as bright and glittering as
when the photograph had caught them, a face
looked out, positively glowing with macabre,
devious humour, with animated interest.

With malice.

Over the rounded head, the barest hint of
feathers. The long face ended in a snout that

appeared like nothing less than a sharp, viciously barbed beak. The chest, what could be seen of it, seemed furred. Powerful shoulders loomed half-hidden by foliage, the all-concealing foliage that had cloaked the dark, terrible form that looked out, even as the girl looked back at the lens.

Ava drew a deep breath.

"It's the gryphon."

"Gryphon? Nonsense. More than nonsense, impossible, it has to be a model, a prop, something the photographer put there. It's a joke; what is it doing there — next to her?"

"Where else would it be? It's not a joke, it's not a model, Cass; I only wish it were! *It's the gryphon*. The man holding that camera is Lewis Carroll. That girl in the picture – that is the same girl we saw at the grave – that, there, is Alice Liddell. *His Alice*."

"I don't give a damn whose 'Alice' she is – gryphons do not exist," he maintained.

"Cass. The fox that you found, the one that you told me about, on the Mount – could a beak have done that?"

He rose and walked away from her – but his eyes returned to the screen.

"Gryphons do not exist, Ava."

She joined him; she, too, stared back at the screen.

"And ghosts *do?*" she said softly. "*We both saw her.* Can you deny it?"

"No, but there has to be another …."

"She wrote on the marble. You saw what she wrote – *and she wrote it in blood. We both saw it.* Can you deny it?"

"No, but, Ava …."

"She is *dead*, Cass."

"I know! I know — I can't explain it! Let's work with something else, something we can understand. Why *you?* What do you have to do with this? How did you see it, how could you possibly make out that *face* in the leaves; no one has ever seen that, *that thing* in this picture before! How did you see it, Ava? Why were you even up there, at that grave?"

She sat slowly on the edge of his bed.

A cloud of horror seemed to hang over his guest. Silent, grave, stiff – she sat on his bed and her mood was so terrible, so full of some dark presage that he shut his mouth. He could not stop himself – he came to sit beside her.

Close enough to touch her, for a second he nearly did, so keen was his sudden fear at what he could only describe as the feeling that radiated from her. She sat there, unmoving. He stayed close to her. They sat, tense – waiting – the two shoulder to shoulder on the bed, united in human need – in a room that had gone strangely colder, somehow more still, a room where apparitions could somehow spring to life.

"I had to go," she explained, finally. "I knew I had to be there. I just knew; don't ask me how. I'm no stranger to her, Cass, to the woman she once was, to that thing at the grave that she is now. *Alice Liddell was my great, great, great grandmother.* But really – what I find most astounding is *you* – why *you?*"

How to tell her without sounding utterly mad? So much of this already is, maybe it no longer matters.

"I saw you, Ava."

"What? Where?"

"You were asleep, on a couch."

"When?"

"A night ago; it was after I found the fox. I wasn't there, I was nowhere near wherever it was you were – *but I saw you, as clearly as I see you right now.* You woke up; you were frightened, like me. You had something in your hand."

She stared at him, aghast. Then, she jumped up. Reaching to her purse on the bed, she finally upended it entirely in her attempts to find something inside. She turned to him and flung it down on the bed – the card – the card of the Queen of Hearts – and all the hearts on the card, as well as the decorations of the Queen herself – were jet black.

"*You.* And *me.* Come on," she cried hoarsely; and she rushed from the room.

Chapter 6

CASTLE HILL

He ran to keep pace with her.

Ava had flown down the stairs. Before he had time to grab his coat and the flashlight, she was already out the door and standing in the street. His cell phone was in his hand; she called back to him.

"Bring it or leave it; it won't matter. It won't work, not where we're going. I've already tried."

Obstinate, he kept the phone.

She led him to the river, crossing at the nearest footbridge. The water was low. It curled languid and dark, as dark as Cass' thoughts. They left the bridge for the eastern shore; he was still grasping for a logical explanation as to how a creature of myth, of legend, might have crossed that same stream.

Is that how that thing crosses, too?

Or does it swim?

Stop it. Gryphons do not exist.

Moonlight lay bright in the empty streets of Guildford. No one marked their passage as they reached High Street, halting outside the Castle grounds.

The main gates were locked. This proved only a minor detail to the girl whose hair gleamed like gold in the night; she found the point in the hedge that she sought. With Cass close behind her, they passed through and entered a realm of wonder.

He had been here many times before. Since his return here a fortnight ago, here he had been continually drawn; here, angry and bereft, he had steadfastly refused to come.

He had never been here at night; now he stood spellbound.

They were in a small copse; ahead lay the ancient tumbled stones. Etched brilliantly by the moon's glow, the scattered ruins were dazzling, surreal. Even in the day, the Castle ruins were richly evocative. Tourists thronged here to dally on history's footpath, eager to see some of the region's finest Saxon ruins.

The remnants of the Castle remained regal and imposing. Even in near obliteration, the intangible aura of the place was undiminished. It had stood for nearly a millennium and all who beheld it felt something of the power and magnetic presence of the past.

This may not have been entirely due to the site's historic provenance.

What had lain beneath those decaying and tumbled stones had been here longer – much longer.

Long before the Lords had raised their keep, an earlier moon had lit a landscape here of mystery and dread. Then, older stars had gleamed coldly down upon an age far more savage, still mystifying, still cryptic. Here had been a place of worship. Long before the coming of the church's drear and listless tenets, on this hill, the festivals were marked. Long before the raising of the sad, impenetrable cross, before the cold litanies that paled beside the richness and power of the old chants – this had been a place of sacrifice.

A millennia ago, here sorcery had held dominion for the very earth beneath the stones and edifice had betokened magic itself.

Portentous dreams, dark and marvelous visions, long life and cures for some, for others the start of swift decline – the power of the Hill was the light and wonder of an age bound in legend.

The legends had not all been forgotten.

While Cass did not know these tales, and would never have paid them even the lip service accorded any modern urban legend, here, in the dark, under a full moon – he suddenly felt a strange pull from the earth at his feet. He sensed without hearing sounds that now echoed faintly in the small copse.

At the edge of perception, voices rose and fell with the night's wind.

They whispered, asking, demanding, in tongues long dead. In wonder, Cass listened, harkening to them, wandering for a split second in their grasp, and in his mind – a door began to open and a reply came unbidden to his lips.

I call the East, the King....

Startled, he looked sharply down at his own hand – there was nothing there.

What did you expect to see?

He shook his head, trying to clear away the sense of vision, of déjà-vu, to find an anchor in present time and place. He forced himself to look about him. Stones lay scattered across the grounds; a simple light played over their pitted surfaces. Yet their contours and expected symmetry seemed odd to him, inconstant, as if photographic images had been laid one over the other. Fractured, somehow less familiar, the light itself seemed uncanny here; soft yet potent, more insistent.

More deadly.

Something is here, something terrible is here.

I have been here before but now, suddenly –

I know this place, how do I know this place?

The pressure of Ava's hand on his arm drew him back again from what was less a reverie than an actual trance.

"It's this way," she murmured.

She led him to the rough border of the largest grove on the far side of the Castle. There, walking under trees whose youth concealed the stark antiquity of the ground that fed their roots, more stones lay. Grey, shattered into smaller bits, yet undiminished, the stones clearly bore the mark of human hands, and Cass' mind reeled.

Here – here is the source – where it comes from, what I am feeling.

These stones; they are not like the others.

Those other stones are tame, shackled, imprisoned by time, by their very destruction.

Not these.

At the heart of what might have been a long, broken, nearly defaced ring of fragments and almost obscured by shadow, the heavy pieces of an ancient altar stone lay before them.

In some nameless past, this stone had been whole. Quarried and carved with care, its thick supports still held much of it above the moist turf. Surrounded and sheltered by the prostate reminders of ages past, the back of the wide center stone had fallen, perhaps under its own weight, with only the vestiges of its side supports keeping it off the ground.

Below the wide stone, rimmed with cobweb and tattered moss, a dark, open space extended.

Ava turned to him. "Watch."

She took a step forward. Before the nearest edge of the flat, lichen-covered altar stone with its gaping shadows below, she knelt down.

Very slowly, her hand reached out, toward the darkness under the stone.

Cass' breath stopped for a moment – for the ground below her hand grew suddenly clearer –

with light. Then, barely seen – as moonlight did not reach this place easily, at least not in this age – the dark space beneath the altar stone's lip seemed to change as well. Pale blue light crept up and over the lip of the stone, coming from below.

But a strange darkness, deeper than the shadows, began to appear in the cramped and angled space below the tipped stone. Slowly and silently – widening until it seemed large enough to admit a person, albeit on all fours – a hole opened in the earth itself.

How did she find this thing?

Ava was now seated on the ground. Her arm and shoulders were trembling, her breath came raggedly, unevenly, as if the hole that grew and grew, extending deeper and deeper into the dark earth, were feeding upon the girl's breath itself.

He knelt beside her. With a cry, she wrenched her hand back, away from the hungry chasm in the loam and leaves. Reaching blindly to take his hand, hers was icy and trembling, beads of sweat were on her white forehead. Leaning forward to peer down, Cass had just enough time to see that the hole spiraled downward in a kind of tunnel.

Soft and blue, the last vestiges of light were still apparent; they rose from inconceivable depths below.

Dizziness swept over him, a wave of profound vertigo – before his eyes, the fissure shimmered again, and the light danced inside as it broke up and faded into reassuring darkness.

The hole was closing up; in moments, the nether depths were lost to view.

All that was left was the grim stone with its cavern, desolate yet not entirely untenanted – and the two, kneeling in some uncanny, perverted reverence – before it.

Ava's held breath was released; it hung visible in the air. She pointed to the earth beside them.

Now, undistracted by the phenomenon of a tunnel opening where a tunnel could not possibly do so, he saw them. He finally turned on his light.

There were marks in the moist earth.

Splayed like so many fingers, they were clearly prints. In any other place, they would have been simply the tracks of wildlife, the expected, harmless night time visitors that frequented this half wild place, neither significant nor interesting.

But this was not just any other place.

There were tracks; there were many. They led to and from the very place where a doorway had opened in the ground, and just as impossibly, had closed; where a young man now sat upon his heels, unable to move, unable to speak – stiff with wonder, agitated, utterly without recourse to explanation.

They were the prints of the thing that did not exist – the tracks of the gryphon.

Chapter 7

WONDER

His aunt said nothing about that night, not about the lateness of the hour of his return to the house or about what had absorbed his time until then.

Much, much later, Cass would wonder at this.

The next morning he found Abby in the solarium; his aunt would always tend her plants before her morning walks. Here, she fostered a formidable collection of orchids and exotic plants, whose fragile needs were at odds with the typical English winter.

He stepped inside, met by a wave of warmth and wet, the heat and high humidity at once soothing and disturbing. He recalled coming here, wandering happily as a child would; it seemed lifetimes ago. Abby looked up and motioned him nearer.

"Look at this, Cass. The orchids are finally blooming – this one is 'Casablanca.' That one is called 'Black Eye Pea' – it's quite lovely. And this bromeliad is the Royal's Tears, or something like that, I think – just look at how the pink stems end in bright blue flowers, such a perfect blue."

Her admiring gaze ranged across the tables with their rich flowers and glossy foliage and she took up her smallest pruning shears, busily engaged in removing dry leaves from the stem of an enormous bloom. Even in this place of safety, held close in an embrace of soft light and warmth, Cass' mind was elsewhere – he was back under dark trees where some kind of hellish mouth had opened nearly under his feet.

He finally spoke, stepping irrevocably across the line that separated doubt from resolution.

"Abby. There's something I need to know. What does our family have to do – with Lewis Carroll?"

Hovering above the orchid, her shears froze in midair.

She did not turn to look at him. Slowly, the shears were lowered, and returned to their place on the long wooden table.

T

Pale late morning light filled the library. Beside the low table near the couch, Abby poured a cup of tea.

Her nephew sat beside her, silent, expectant.

For some moments, she studied the cup's gilded edge and the nearly transparent porcelain catching the light. In the amber liquid at the cup's bottom, tea leaves revolved, taking on fantastic shapes.

Without speaking, she looked straight at Cass, holding his eyes with hers. She rose and walked to the library windows, and once more, Abigail Hythe looked out onto her gardens. Once more, as if in final assent, her eyes were drawn to the old gate that led up to the Mount.

The Mount.

Where he lies.

She turned to her nephew.

"I'll tell you; on one condition. First, that you tell me *the truth* – what is on the Mount that has so absorbed you, these last few days? The truth, Cass."

"The truth?" he wondered. "The truth is something I can no longer presume with certainty. I doubt that you would believe me, Abby. No one would."

Something was in her gaze – in its directness, its steadiness – he hurried on.

"Alright. I found something up there. I learned something that has to do with the killings, here in Guildford. The killings…."

His aunt's hand came up.

"No! That's quite enough." She turned away, struggling for a moment, it seemed.

Is she angry? No. She's afraid of something.

She went to the desk, taking the old journal from the drawer. She returned to him, putting it into his hands.

"This was my father's journal – your grandfather's, Cass. I've marked the pages for you."

"Marked the pages? What pages?"

She sat beside him. She motioned to the book; Cass began to read. Page after page turned. A stream of widely varied emotions crossed his face, from wonder, through doubt, to stupefaction.

Finally, slowly, he closed the book. He studied its cover. His long fingers played over the age- softened leather. He placed the book on the table before him, looking up to find that his aunt was gazing at him appraisingly.

"Is that the writing of a mad man, Cass? Do you think he was mad?"

"No. No; I remember grandfather. He wasn't mad; I know he was young when he wrote this, but he wasn't mad. I'm not mad, either. I found its tracks, up on the Mount, Abby. I found what it killed up there. I haven't actually *seen* the thing – but, I have seen the grave. I've seen a little girl. *And now – the hole, itself.* There's no doubt in my mind. What's in that journal, what grandfather was trying to relate about what his own father had told him – I haven't a doubt in the world, anymore. I believe it. I think that Carroll actually went *below*."

She let out a long breath.

"There have been times, Cass, when I questioned my own sanity. It was so long ago, it seemed like a dream. When the call came to my grandfather – to come to the house, to listen to a dying man – that was the day my father was writing about. Carroll told him about his – journey – *under*. That book, that children's story – that 'thing' he concocted for the Liddell children, it was nothing more than that. *A concoction.* I find it amusing, amazing even – that what entertained those children, and has delighted all the world, since, it seems – actually kept the man from completely losing his mind. He turned it into a fairy tale; it was very clearly anything but. Carroll exacted a promise from my grandfather, that he would do what was necessary – when the time came."

"Do what was necessary? *You mean, go there himself?* But my grandfather didn't go *under, either,* did he?"

"No, he didn't. I think he was afraid, too afraid. You see, he believed the story, too."

"But Abby …..."

She rose and paced.

"I know, I know – and it was a deathbed promise. My father never kept it. *Neither did your father.* It wasn't kept in your father's time either, even though Randolph *knew* it had been promised. Cass, your father read that journal himself; I can say with certainty that he believed it. But he had a family, he had responsibilities; he thought – I don't know what he thought. He made a choice, he chose *not* to go. *Then it began all over again, the killings started again, in your own father's time."*

"My God," said Cass.

The grandfather wouldn't, the father – he couldn't…..

In his mind, he saw a playing card with all its hearts jet-black, as black as the eyes that had stared out, greedily, tauntingly into his. "It's really back, Abby, the gryphon is back. It's come back up, the proof was there, up on the Mount. I found it again, just last night – at the portal itself."

Her head lowered, and her voice went down to whisper.

"I had so wished … but, no. Now I wonder; I wonder."

Taking up the journal, Cass rose and went to the windows. He, too, looked out at the gardens – and at the little gate.

"I know what you're wondering, Abby. It's what I'm wondering. Can it be any more necessary – than now? If someone doesn't go – what happens next? *What gets killed next – if 'what's necessary' isn't finally done?"*

She went to him and took the book from his hands.

"I can't answer this for you. You're a man now. It's no longer for me to tell you what to do, what must be done. But, I can tell you I'm afraid, Cass. I'm afraid for us all – but how very much more afraid I am – for you."

༈

"I have to do this."

"No. You don't," he insisted.

"Yes, I do. What else can I do? What other course of action is possible, Cass? I'm listening."

He had no answer for the young woman sitting across from him at the pub, with her hair gleaming in the thin autumn sunshine.

Earlier that afternoon, when she had returned from her walk, Abby had found her nephew once more in the library. This time, he had not been alone; the aunt had smiled at seeing the stunning, red haired beauty with him. That aunt had unexpectedly embraced the nephew and, with bright eyes, had eagerly shaken hands with his visitor, again asking no question – other than to enquire after the fair guest's birth date. It seemed no great surprise that the two young people were going out to the pub. Neither had she raised an eyebrow at his request for an early dinner. But she had watched them from the open door as they had made their way toward the village – and the smile had gone from her face.

The pub was crowded, and noisy and happy. The two at the corner table were wholly oblivious to all of it. Ava tapped restless fingers on her glass. She was waiting to hear the plan, the real plan, the plan other than the obvious one, the one that Cass or any other sane person under normal circumstances might justify offering.

No plan came.

"Think for a minute, Cass. What would the police say, what would anyone say, if we presented them with this?"

He made a vague, non-committal snort about long therapy sessions.

"I'm going in," she repeated.

"Ava …"

"No, I'm going to do this. I'm going underground. I think I have to. *I'm supposed to.* That *thing* does it – it clearly goes in and out. Why not me? I'm going in, and I'm going to get to the bottom of this."

He finished his drink.

"Bad pun, Fitzalan. But, no – you're *not* going in. *We are.*"

They spoke for a long time; there was a lot to say and even more not to say, for suddenly things seemed to have changed. Then, they parted, in a perverse kind of grim accord as to what must happen next. Cass left the pub, so absorbed in what was going through his mind that he had no clear recollection of taking the long way home, crossing the Wye, turning up the Guilddown Road to finally reach the lawns and wide stone porch of the Hythe residence.

It was all a whirl – the events of the past few days; a fox ripped apart, a face impossibly alive on a laptop screen, an altar stone with an awful and uncanny secret beneath it. Finally, there was now the insane prospect of attempting to penetrate the mystery firsthand. Yet he was a reasonable man and therefore torn – to proceed or not proceed? It was madness, either way. At no point in his journey did he stop vacillating; at least not until he had the house in sight and started up the leaf strewn stone path leading to the door.

It was there that his indecision vanished.

Like a man struck by lightning, Cass stared down. He stood on dirt as familiar, as ordinary as common dirt could be. Across the yard, a cold wind blew more dry leaves, lifting those on the path; they rustled, skittering like so many sere, brown hands clutching at his shoes. Yet, when the wind had died down and the walk itself was cleared, his heart hammered in his chest.

His purpose might still be in doubt, but his resolve was clear.

There, below him, at the very door of the place where his only existing family lived in suddenly tenuous safety – lay a present, the token of a recent visitor.

It was wet, glistening, as simple and as grimly mocking as might be a thrown gauntlet – with a newly severed hand still inside. It lay in plain sight, as disdainfully in plain sight as had been a face that had stared out of some innocent foliage, captured in an archaic, time-worn photograph, still animated by dreadful life.

A pretty little present; freshly torn from yet another hapless victim – there in the dirt lay a heart.

It lay at his very door, and beside it, as foully crimson as was the heart itself – was the track of the gryphon.

Ŧ

It started as well as it could.

While Cass was out, Ava had appeared early at their doorstep for supper; with her was a light knapsack, uncannily similar to the one that, with some difficulty, he had returned to leave readied by the front door.

> *How do you prepare for something like this?*
> *What do you bring?*
> *What do you bring with you if – just possibly*
> *– you might be going to Hell?*

Dinner was finally finished. Abby's nephew unexpectedly held her close, and she herself did not let Ava leave without an embrace. However, there was a strange look in her eyes as she watched them wordlessly prepare to leave the house, looking more like burglars than lovers.

This was a woman grounded, skilled and faithful. Yet a sensation had been growing since the early part of the day. Now, at the last, again it had hit her – a feeling of dread promptly overtook the mistress of the house just as the door had closed behind them.

So overpowering was the feeling of portent that she rushed after them, flinging the door open in a mad attempt to call them back.

The light of the full moon, at once sobering and ominous, cascaded across the stone paved porch, and leaves pranced in the breeze. But Abigail Hythe stood in her doorway, trembling for no reason that she could name, seeking a solace that might now never come.

Except for the moon above and the mournful sound of the wind in the trees, she stood there alone.

It was too late.

They were already gone.

Ŧ

"Are you sure about the phone?"

"I tried," she said. "More than once; the closer you get to this thing, the faster the signal goes haywire."

She extinguished her torch. Awash in ribbons of moonlight, with her hair ruffled by the wind and her cheeks flushed, Cass regarded Ava as she stood by the altar stone.

Anywhere but here – in just this kind of moonlight – I want to see her just like this.

Anywhere but here.

She took her eyes off the altar stone and looked at him suddenly.

"Cass – what do you think it is – really? I've been going over in my mind what you said earlier; it does make some crazy kind of sense."

"I hear a 'but' hanging there somewhere," he said.

"You know it," she said, and shivered.

He shivered too; both of them were warmly dressed. But they stood before the altar stone; again, the earth seemed to pull at them. He, too, extinguished his light and they waited for their eyes to meet the dark.

"I think it's some kind of spatial rift. A hole that can somehow open, that has opened into our own world. It must be a portal. For the rest of it – what actually controls the thing, why you seem to be able to make it do this, and what I have to bring to the table – I haven't a clue. Why the gryphon can go in and out of that hole is beyond me."

She knelt down, scrutinising the stone's moss encrusted edge.

"And gryphons do not exist? Maybe they do exist – down there," she said.

Laughter burst from him. The idea of the two of them deliberately crawling into some kind of unpredictably unstable hyperspace was suddenly ludicrous, as mad as the possibility – the real probability – that imaginary animals might also be able to exist in that space.

There was no chance to argue the absurdity of any of it. Without warning – Ava leaned forward

– her bare hand reached into the space below the stone.

It came instantaneously this time.

Eagerly, voraciously, from deep within the cobweb – limned space beneath the massive altar, it rose. As if in welcome answer to a dreadful summons – pale blue light welled up.

This time it was torrential, billowing like a stream. Pulsing and swirling, now it coursed toward them, up past the lip of the stone and before Cass could move, the fingers of the girl at his feet were bathed in sapphire. With a cry, Ava plunged in her other hand; it, too, floated in luminescence.

The portal responded – icy now, the air itself bent, moving in his sight, crackling and roaring.

In a sudden surge, radiance erupted up and outward from the space beneath the looming altar. Then, growing out of its very heart – a chasm less black than the utter absence of light ripped open, gaping steadily wider and deeper.

He tumbled down beside her and seized her arm. At his contact with the girl, the light spilled forward, enfolding him as well and the iridescent air rippled and tore. His flesh crawled, stinging, as though raked by icy claws.

Cass' hair lifted in a frigid wind, one that moaned, for now surely, there was a kind of voice there, under the deafening resonance of chaos. Her own hair floating, the face of the girl beside him convulsed in terror.

He could no longer see anything. His senses were torn, as wildly uncontrollable as the fear that lashed at him – as above the lip of the stone, a symbol, as clear as if carved from glacial ice, coalesced, taking on awful life seemingly out of the tortured air itself. One by one, five shadowy squares took form. Joined at the center, a square that was not a square floated, measureless, ever changing. The sides were innumerable now and the quincunx in all its parts began to rotate, its sides folding and unfolding in upon themselves, and words began to form in Cass' mind.

And in the twelfth part, there shall I be, and there shall Thy Sign be also.

He fell forward into a vacuum, a nothingness that was limitless, without dimension. A searing blast of heat and cold and voices howling in anger curled over him – then both the light and girl were swept from his sight.

Chapter 8

LAND

"Cass."

The voice was low and right at his ear.

He opened his eyes. A side-ways view of the world was all he saw; it was a dark world, blurred and indistinct.

Your face is in the dirt – smell it.

Yes, it's dirt.

Dirt; real dirt. Or is it?

"Can you hear me?" Ava asked. "Cass. Do something. Can you just nod or maybe spit, or something?"

Nausea still gripped him. But he managed to roll onto his back. His hands rubbed his aching temples. He hauled himself up onto his knees and regarded her. She regarded him back.

"Which would you prefer, Fitz?" he asked.

Her eyes lit. "Fitz. Why did you call me that?"

He reached across to pluck a stray dead leaf from her shoulder. "Don't know; seemed right."

She dragged him up onto his feet, and dusted him off. "It was my dad's pet name for me."

Her voice told him immediately that the man was no more, and how much he was missed; at his penetrating look, she lowered her eyes.

"You, too?" he asked softly. "But, how did you….?"

"Remember dinner, about a hundred years ago? You'd gone to get another bottle of wine. That was when Abby told me."

"I wonder," he interrupted. "Why did she tell you?"

"Strange that you mention it – I didn't notice at the time. She did; no reason given. But look, we have each other now, here in this charming place. You can't imagine how charming it is. See? I do *so* hope that counts for something, yet – down here?"

He looked about him. He, too, began to fervently hope that it counted for something, as well.

With its surface of scattered twigs and dead leaves, the packed earth they stood on seemed common enough. But the large cave that extended around them had no distinct borders and pale light still shimmered down from a wide tunnel over their heads.

Of the roof and walls that could be seen, twisted, densely interlocking tree roots formed a thick meshwork. Evidence of their new world's true nature lay hanging on the walls – spider webs, most impossibly massive, and many apparently recent. It was the size of the webs, and the thickness of their silks that made Cass frown. Loose stones and boulders lay scattered about the hard soil at their feet.

But away from the hole, in the near distance, the chamber changed dramatically, the natural earthen floor giving way to something utterly unexpected.

No longer dark, fetid earth but an intricately laid floor of fantastically decorated tiles appeared. The tiles spread, wall-to- wall, down a long corridor whose wood paneled walls were lined by seemingly endless doors.

Slinging her pack across her shoulder, Ava left him. She halted at the border between dirt and tile, studying the edge where earth became ceramic, as if uneasy about her next step. After a long moment, she stepped across to stand fully on the marvelous floor. His own pack in hand, Cass followed her. Yet when he looked back behind him, toward the spot they had just left, he exhaled in wonder.

From this vantage, the space they had just left – was no longer as it had been just seconds ago. Gone was the chamber of darkly shadowed earth and tree root. In its place was a limitless, utterly dark void, without form, without even the light that had cascaded dimly, but somehow comfortingly from above, where the tunnel's path to the upper world must have been.

He turned on his torch, sending its light darting across the space. There was nothing. The room of earth and leaves was gone.

So is the way out.

Ava was staring into the dark as well; two anxious gazes met.

"Trail of bread crumbs?" she muttered weakly.

"GPS would be preferable."

She laughed suddenly, her voice loud and strange in the queer space. "Good luck with that," she said. "But, Cass, look here."

She left him again, this time approaching one of the doors that lined the silent hallway. Every one of the doors was beautifully carved. Every one of the doors was different, and from around and below their frames – every single one of them – pale light curled out, mist-like, cold and menacingly, feeling its way into the corridor.

In the hall before the nearest door, a wide, sturdy, yet cleanly fashioned wooden table stood.

There were no other furnishings.

Except for the luminescence of the mist, the corridor seemed dark at its end, and always, in the space at their backs, thick darkness reigned. Cass stared back into that darkness, and the hair lifted on his neck.

"Fitz. There's something back there; back there in the dark," he said at last. Ava's eyes were also rapt on the space that held no tangible evidence of anything at all.

"I know. Whatever it is, I hope it stays there."

She tore her eyes away from the dark and its unseen menace and went to the table. On the wide surface of polished, inlaid wood – there was a small box of dark metal. Cass joined her.

"Wait," he said. Then he reached for what might be the box's lid. The moment his hand touched it – the box lid opened – to reveal another box inside, this one just as dark against a lining of pure gold. With another touch – came another box within.

"Is this some kind of joke?" Ava muttered. "If it is – it's not funny."

"Not a joke. It's part of the game," he said. "We have to do what comes next."

She stared at him now. "Why, exactly – and what game?"

He looked past her into the darkness then back at the box. "I suspect – the game that will finally lead us out of here. What did Alice find on the table?"

His next touch proved useless – the box within stayed closed. Ava drew near.

"What Alice found on the table – was a key."

Her fingers touched the box – it opened – to reveal a golden key; they studied the bright little thing.

"'Find the Servant; turn the Key'," she said. "Is this the Key? Do I pick it up?" she asked.

"What did *Alice* do?" Cass wondered.

"What, indeed?" came a low voice.

They whirled around – the voice had come from inside the dark space behind them, reverberating as if from far away. The source of the voice was terrifying enough. Its *sound* was what drove the two away from the table, to put some kind of solid wall at their backs. Low, resonant, the voice was rasping, like the keening sound of sighing and again, the hair on Cass' neck stirred.

Like something sighing in the dark.

Like an animal – sighing in the dark.

Ava's fingers tightened on his arm; she was staring into the shadows. Her jaw set and she gave a low cry. When he followed her gaze, he quickly shoved her behind him, for out of the dark, where once simple root and familiar earth had been, something terrible and unaccountable had appeared.

Starting from some great distance away, two blood-red eyes shone out – they were exactly what he had seen on his computer screen, that night in his room and this time – they hung in space more than four feet above the point where should have been the ground. This time, they were coming closer and closer, directly toward them.

Chapter 9

CHOOSE A SKIN

"I said… what, indeed?"

The speaker stood before them.

As large as a dog, it stood poised on its hind legs, legs that were furred in white, but with patches missing from parts of the long limbs.

"It can't be," breathed Cass.

"I am not going to listen to you anymore," whispered his companion. "That's what you said about the gryphon."

"A *rabbit?*"

It was a Rabbit; but like neither of them had seen before. This one stood on its hind legs, as easily as a man might. This one was dressed in the tattered remnants of a waistcoat, and was carrying what appeared to be a long, ebony walking stick.

The creature clutched a pair of folded, faded white gloves in one of its paws, paws that were sickeningly like human hands, albeit with long, sharp nails. Its ragged, yellow claws clicked on the tiles as the thing walked past them to the table, where it placed its gloves and stick. The two humans drew back as the animal unexpectedly turned a long, white- furred face to them.

The crimson eyes that Cass had seen looming out of the darkness of his computer screen had been horrible; they were infinitely more so with the creature's face attached.

Brilliant red, now they shone out in the low light of the corridor and the Rabbit, if rabbit it was, peered at them with a curiously chilling look, full of anticipation.

Full of malice.

It has the same look in its eyes, as we saw in the eyes of the gryphon in the photograph.

Is this the same creature?

A low snarl erupted from the thing's lips.

"Pay attention," warned the low, keening voice. When the Rabbit spoke, its teeth showed beneath its whiskered lips, and those teeth were savagely sharp and brilliant white in the gloom.

"So! You are here at last. It certainly took you long enough," said the Rabbit to Ava. "I told Gryphon to stop; *enough* with the cats and dogs. He needed to kill a *child* next – that would certainly get you down here right quick. Yet He was not keen on it; not at all. Can't say why; the idea doesn't bother me in the least."

The creature chuckled; it was a ghastly sound.

"I think the gryphon found a better way," murmured Cass. Then, he stiffened. The thing that should have been simply Alice's 'Little White Rabbit', with neat waistcoat and gloves, had turned its glaring attention to him.

"Who … is *that?* And why have you brought him here?" the Rabbit hissed at the girl.

Cass' blood warmed unexpectedly at this; his chin came up.

"She didn't *bring* me. I came."

"Whatever for?"

"To see the job was done."

The animal's lip curled into a vicious smile, and it took a short step closer.

"*How kind.* But how utterly unnecessary. She doesn't need any of *your* help. Don't you see? She's perfectly capable of getting herself killed here, all by herself. So! You should leave. Right now!" The thing waved a paw at him, dismissively. "You can go back up safely, right now, if you like."

Cass gave a short laugh. "Don't be an ass. I'm not going anywhere – not without her."

His words had a devastating effect, for the look in the eyes of the tall anomaly changed in a flash. Gone was cool appraisal; furious rage had taken its place. With jaws agape and white teeth gnashing, the beast took a threatening step toward the human.

That human held his ground – the Rabbit halted. Cass wondered, for his adversary's whiskers had begun to twitch.

He's not quite sure of me. Well, now.

He cast a quick glance at his companion. The Rabbit, too, turned to her.

"*She* won't be pleased, you know," the thing snarled at Ava.

"I don't give a damn if *She* is or not," she replied mildly. Ava was calm, immobile; it was Cass who was unnerved, for it was clear to him at last of whom they spoke.

It's the Queen.

He means the Queen.

So does Ava.

His mind was filled with the memory of the Queen, with Her dark eyes, livid face, with Her red raiment turning ebony before his eyes. As though the creature followed his thoughts, the Rabbit glared again at him. Yet, it seemed that it glared impotently.

He won't stop us. Or he can't.
It's part of the game, and he knows it.

The Rabbit sniffed fastidiously; it turned away.

"So be it," it sneered. It picked up the golden key from the box on the table, and tossed it to the floor at their feet.

"Leave it, Cass," Ava warned; he had been just about to kneel to retrieve the key.

Thin wisps of pale mist or smoke began to rise from the key although the metal itself seemed unchanged. Ava turned to the Rabbit and it laughed malevolently.

"Good girl! Bright girl! It's wise to keep your wits about you, here. Think – think hard before you act. Or all too soon, you may never be able to act at all."

"Where is the 'lake of tears'?" demanded Ava suddenly; the Rabbit's eyes sparkled with pleasure.

"Tears will come soon enough. Be ready," it replied.

"And now?" she asked.

"You know the way, or soon you will!" The Rabbit's clawed hand waved at their garments. "But you can't go anywhere like that. Not here! Choose! *Choose a skin.*"

Cass scowled.

"What do you mean – 'choose a skin'?"

The Rabbit's eyes brightened. Now they fairly glowed with unholy red light, as if its orbs were lit from within by live coals. The creature's words came low and fast, but they echoed in the hall, and for a second, Cass wasn't actually sure what he was seeing – was it indeed a rabbit, or something else – that spoke through the creature before them?

> *"Choose a skin!*
> *Quickly come and choose the skin,*
> *That will set the role you're in.*
> *All must play – don't ask me why.*
> *Choose a skin – to live or die!"*

Ava paled. "He means we must choose a *form,* one that we will wear in … this place."

"A form? What form? You mean a character? We have to choose a character? Was that in the story?" whispered Cass.

The Rabbit broke in.

"You thought you knew the story, didn't you? But stories change all the time; they've changed here. *Choose.*"

Cass's jaw set. "What if we don't?"

The Rabbit's sharp teeth seemed longer and so much sharper as it grinned. "Ah! Well, then! If you do not choose – then, here you stay."

Cass turned; he did not see the look of wicked triumph in the infernal animal's eyes.

"I'll choose," Ava exclaimed.

The Rabbit gloated. "Excellent!"

"I choose… *Chevalière,*" she said and for a moment, such was the hatred on the Rabbit's face that both humans tensed.

"You… *dare* …." it stammered.

"I do! I dare! I choose *Chevalière – the Knight. I'm not done*. How many times may we change again – before the end?" she demanded.

Death was in the Rabbit's eyes; the creature fairly spat the words at her.

*"You may each change again – **once!***

But – only once!

*And I will not say for how long – but for **now** – Chevalière it is!"*

Its voice was a shout – the creature's eyes blazed cold and suddenly blue.

The air around Ava Fitzalan grew dense, until Cass could no longer see her. Dizzy, his own vision blurred – then suddenly, he could again see the face and form of the young woman before him.

There she stood, as he might only have dared to imagine her.

She was garbed head to foot in fine leather, from the Knight's short, close fitting jerkin that covered her finely woven linen shirt, to the sturdy boots on her feet. The Chelavière's breeches were umber and fit her closely, revealing the taut suppleness of her limbs. Protecting her arms from wrist to elbow were leather vambraces and their bright metal studs caught the light even in the tunnel's dim anteroom. Gone was her knapsack; a light leather bag replaced it, hanging at her belt.

The new-made Knight's gloved hand pushed back a dark green cloak overlaid with a design of small black hearts. Cass saw her weapons: dagger, short sword and at her belt – a finely worked white ivory baton, like a wand.

Brilliant!

She's carrying enough for a real fight.

But will that be enough – here?

And do the skills come with the boots?

The beast turned blazing red eyes upon him. "Now – you!"

He was nonplussed for a second. Then, in a flash, it came to him; he had his choice.

"I choose *The Red Joker – the Knave.* Yes, an American card."

The Rabbit's eyes widened; then it lowered its head in a queer salute. Again came the flash of deepest blue from the animal's eyes, again the wave of faintness. When it had cleared, Cass looked down on himself.

He stood now in black and red foolscap, his leggings smooth and tight over his thighs. Over a midnight black shirt, the short cloak displayed the red and black patchwork of the harlequin, adorned and flourished in alternating black and red hearts.

He, too, had a baton at his belt – but his was the same kind of wand pictured in Abby's ancient Tarot deck. Beside it, a leather bag hung, just as it had appeared on the card. In it would be all the tokens of the remaining suits, pentacles, cups and wands and Cass was supremely grateful for a conversation he had had just days ago. For, with a mind toward possibly unimaginable events, Cass had questioned his aunt, at length, about every single one of the cards in the major card suits of the deck he had taken from the drawer.

Abby's words still rang in his mind:

'The Joker, Cass, is also called the Knave. Look at it, look at it carefully. The Joker is a powerful card, so very powerful, in many ways one of the strongest,' she had said. 'The Tarot tells the story of the Soul's journey to enlightenment – from level to level of awareness, of power – of risk. How does the Joker begin? Look to the oldest decks – he

first appears as the Mountebank, the performer, the trickster, the charlatan, even. But listen, Cass – The Knave does not remain the Mountebank. The Joker does not stay the Joker. He becomes the Magus – the Magician, the Sorcerer who draws his power from above. But I warn you, Cass; I warn you. That power can be prodigious – it can be consuming. It is always deadly – for power is all.'

The young man adjusted his own gloves hanging at this belt and the Rabbit surveyed its work.

Its grim smile was momentary; a faint noise arose out of the dark behind it. Low and indistinct though it was, still the creature roused and the Rabbit peered back, looking intently – into the shadows.

"My, my! How very late it is; as sure as ferrets are ferrets. I should know – for I do *so* love ferrets, and I am not alone in that! But shall I … or the Duchess … be savage if I've kept *Her* waiting?"

Still at the edge of hearing but nearer, the sound came again. Rapt, the Rabbit's dreadful eyes searched the darkness, and those eyes suddenly widened and its whiskers made a violent twitch.

Without another word, it snatched up its gloves and stick. Quickly pacing to the nearest door in the corridor, it opened it, and disappeared inside.

There was no opportunity to follow it.

From the black null space, a horrifying cry came.

It was the cry of an animal. Ringing with terrible pain and fear, it was a cry as sharp, as grisly and so alike to the sound of the fox in its last moments that the Knave grimaced.

Silence descended; it was soon broken. Drawing ever nearer, eerie sounds of soft, padding footsteps reached the Knight and the Knave.

Without a moment's hesitation, the hand of the girl turned Chevalière flew to her scabbard. Masterfully, she drew out her bright, new sword – and brandished it unerringly and directly at the thing that was coming inexorably closer.

For, rising out of the dark – another voice came, one whose words made up a deep, chanting speech.

Chapter 10

GRYPHON

This voice was deeper than that of the Rabbit, its tones melodic and softer.

Yet, still alien; a horrific medley of sounds drifted toward them and louder now came the padding footsteps and the clicking of talons until the creature stepped into view.

The girl turned Knight had every appearance of calm; the young man could scarcely contain his wonder. For, there in plain sight, finally, was the creature that did not exist – the Gryphon.

Larger than a puma, it was longer and much more massive. Sporting long, upright ears, a thing half eagle, half lion was paces away. The copper feathers of the head and breast merged seamlessly into a short pelt that extended the length of the animal's body to its hindquarters. Scales graced the front of its legs and forepaws, paws that took the form of bird-like claws with long sharp talons at their tips.

The creature stopped before them, and nonchalantly sat down upon its haunches. Even still, the crest of its feathered head reached waist high. A sharply curved beak – tainted with fresh blood – clacked softly.

Its large eyes, copper and green, and sparkling with intelligence, coolly yet attentively took in the humans, who started when the creature unexpectedly flicked open and then folded its wings, wings that were more than two meters wide at full extension.

The Gryphon's gaze passed from Ava to Cass and back again; then it rose to its feet. With its talons clicking on the tiles, it padded past them; the extensive tail, forked at the tip, lashed back and forth. It stopped at the table, as had the Rabbit, and its gaze returned to the Knight.

"I see he's given you the Key," it said, regarding the gold thing still at Ava's feet. Warbling, growling, musical and wondrous, the Gryphon's voice rang in the hall.

"He has, my Lord," replied Ava.

"You may pick it up – it's quite safe, now, I imagine."

The Knight slowly retrieved the key. It stayed in her hand as she examined it, then it went into her jerkin pocket. The Gryphon's eyes fixed on Cass.

"So. You did come, after all," it remarked.

"I did. I had to," answered the Knave.

"Of course you did. I wish I'd been here to see *his* face – when he saw *you!*"

The Gryphon positively chortled; it was an amazing sound, somewhere between a lion's purr and the high, screaming call of a very large bird of prey. The creature that did not exist studied the Chevalière – her defiant stance, her dagger, the ivory wand with its silver runes – and its liquid gaze lingered on the finely- honed edge of the sword in her hand. Another low, warbling purr came from the feathered throat.

"You chose very well," the beast observed. Its massive head turned back to Cass. "Do you know why *he* was so savage – at her choice?"

Cass shook his head; the creature waited for Ava to respond.

"In the older decks, there was no Queen card. There was only the 'Chevalier', the Knight. And the

Knight was not always - male," she said in a low voice.

The Gryphon chuckled again. Then it paced, turning round and round, making a great circle, lashing its tail, so pleased was it by this idea.

"Do you see? The 'Chevalier' – *became* the Queen," came its low, enigmatic chant. "Now, Lady, you have all the weapons you need; as well as a few you do not yet realise. More are to come; will you be ready for them? Yet, we shall see if the wand serves *you* as well as it did … well."

The Gryphon sighed, leaving the sentence tantalisingly underscored, if incomplete. Cass tensed once more under those uncanny eyes, for the thing suddenly padded closer. It stopped and sat down again – directly in front of him.

Shaken by the presence of the killer, so close – the young man took a very deep breath.

Then, he too, sat down, cross-legged and nearly eye to eye with the thing. Pewter dark and gold, like polished horn, the razor sharp beak was less than a meter from his face – the Knave could smell the fresh blood on its tip.

When the beast's enormous eyes sought and held his, the Joker did not look away.

Instead, he looked deeply into the marvelously brilliant orbs. The moment he did so, the young man began to lose his bearings. Soon, all sense of his surroundings was lost. To all appearances, it did not seem to trouble him that the corridor of doors, the fantastically dressed young woman beside him – all had become dim. In moments, Cass was hardly aware of their existence, barely hearing the breathing of the creature before him. His own breath slowed, deepened, and virtually stopped.

Lost in the green and copper depths of those alien eyes, another vision had slowly opened to Cass' sight. What he heard was and yet was not the Gryphon's voice, and a kind of dialogue began.

'Gryphons do not exist,' said the young Knave – the young Mage.

'Perhaps it is you, young Mage – who do not exist, down here?' came the soft reproof that floated into his mind. 'But do not question existence. Instead – look – look .....'

Somehow Cass turned. Entranced, it seemed to him that he was standing in a garden. It was one whose borders could not be seen, and he was crowded close, surrounded by green things that stirred and murmured softly; everywhere distortion reigned, all that he beheld was profaned by the cloud of death. Pushing past savage, angry blooms and heavy, clutching vines, Cass made his way forward. His flesh crawled, for this was not a place of peace, or one of safety – hidden away at the centre of rich, green splendor, it lay before him – a menace incomprehensible, dreadful.

'Flowers. Their scent is wrong, all wrong.'

'Not wrong,' the Gryphon replied. 'Just different. But keep your eyes open – keep them open wide – do not sleep, Mage.'

Cass stumbled, for, indeed, he was nearly dreaming, slipping into deep slumber; warm, inviting, entrancing.

"Deadly! Do not sleep, Mage – Look!"

He did as the voice commanded, looking beyond the terrible perversions of bloom and leaf, past the parodies of blossoms, whose mouths were wide and ringed with bloody teeth, past soaring stalks from whose livid blooms angry flames threatened to erupt, past the great sunflowers whose many seeds bore the terrible images of living things, bound by terror and torment, helpless in eternal anguish, their voices pleading, resounding in misery, misery….

He looked up and his heart quailed. For there, hidden, then revealed then hidden again, only glimpsed at the edge of cognition – something waited. Within the deepest heart of the garden, it strode; creator and created, essence and source. Horrible, in silence, in utter dominion, a figure walked there. It was cloaked in power and shadow, and the sight filled him with dread. Cass struggled, fighting the vision that lured, even as it repelled.

> *'No,' he said. 'No! I won't.'*
> *'You must. You will,' said the Gryphon.*
> *'Hearken, Mage, hearken, while there is yet time! Listen – and remember….*
> *"You'll pass through Her garden and see to your woe,*
> *How flowers and pathways have all turned to foe.*

Heed the voice in the Seed – do take care how you tread!
For the vines may cause sleep which can never be shed.
But the path you must try, though the peril be green.
Do not look in Her eye! Seek the Truth that's unseen."

Still bound in vision, transfixed, the Knave looked down – his cloak and jerkin were gone. In their place were somber robes, and a star-like radiance floated about the wand -like baton at his belt. In the air before him was the quincunx, the symbol he had seen as the portal had ripped open to claim them. As it swirled slowly, a glowing outline took sudden form on his hand – and a ring appeared.

With a deep, sobbing exhalation, Cass found himself on his hands and knees, back on the tiled floor.

He looked up. The Gryphon's face was directly before his own, the creature regarding him closely. The Knave drew back then clambered up onto his feet. Unsteadily, still caught up and

110

mastered by what he had seen, he turned his back on the Gryphon and walked away.

The creature's eyes had never left him – now it watched him avidly, as Cass, all unheeding, stood lost in a place apart. The Gryphon's gaze narrowed, then suddenly its eyes gleamed. Silently it slid forward, padding after the Knave – then it crouched low.

Without warning, it lunged after Cass. Its sharp, open beak was aimed squarely at the young man's ankle.

In a flash, Ava leapt forward. With the side of her blade, she struck the animal hard on its flank. The Gryphon turned aside and as lightly as a cat, it sprang to the table and leapt up onto it, extending its wings wide.

The creature's eyes flashed imperiously and Cass and Ava stopped where they stood, in awe of the thing on the table. Deadly yet regal, it spoke.

"Behold! You have mastered the second challenge – the paradox inherent in both good and evil, the mystery at the heart of fact. I was alive long before *he* ever thought to write about me. I will survive him – even his memory. Yet do you not find it ever marvelous – how form must follow function? Even the face that we are forced to wear, to put on and then show to the world, the face that is strange to us? Substance is so much more than mere structure. *We are formed by what we do. We are bound by what we are. All comes at a price – but you must use what you have, use it – however the danger, whatever the loss. What you have brought here, what you carry with you – use it – or die.* You asked about the tears, Lady. Now, they come."

With that, the creature furled its wings. Harsh and discordant, a scream burst from its gaping maw. It jumped down from the table and bounded off, back into the darkness and the hand that held the sword shook.

Sound reached them, sound that drew their eyes away, to the very end of the corridor of closed doors.

There at the furthest end of the hall, from around the frames of the doors just visible in the shadows – dark water had begun to seep.

"The Tears! Water – the doors!" Ava exclaimed.

In seconds, water was spreading across the corridor floor. An endless stream surged from around and under the doors, doors whose wood had begun to creak with the enormous weight of water that clearly lay behind them. The water began to foam and seemed to coalesce about itself – a liquid wall of water began to form at the corridor end, building higher and higher, stopped in its advance by nothing they could see. Then, without warning – the wave that rose nearly from floor to ceiling – began to move forward.

"Run!" Cass shouted, for the din of moving water was deafening.

"This way!" she cried.

Then the Knight ran to the very door through which the Rabbit had passed – and turned the brass knob.

Chapter 11

UNDINE

Nothing happened. Ava turned the knob hard, repeatedly – the door remained firmly locked.

"Damn," she cried and in a rage, she struck the door with her gloved fist. This time it rattled mightily in its jamb – it did not open, but where her blow had landed, a deep crack had now appeared in the wood's fine surface.

It wasn't enough; from the far end of the corridor, the wall of water advanced.

"The Key," he cried. "Try the Key!"

She pulled it from her pocket. Yet at the approach of the Key to the keyhole, a great arc of sparks now erupted and floated angrily around the golden thing. Ava dropped it; steam rose from the Key on the floor where it lay in a sheer puddle of water; the girl retrieved it.

"It doesn't work, why doesn't it work? Cass, don't you have anything that would open a door?"

There came a nerve jolting crash of water and then an eerie silence and they stared down the hall.

The wave, massive, still mounting, impossibly like a tidal wave that roiled and surged had paused, hovering in mid air – now suddenly, it swept rapidly forward and Cass stared at it as it thundered toward them.

"Water doesn't move like that!" he insisted angrily.

"It does here," she cried. "And here – it can kill us!"

"Screw the Key," he shouted. With his booted foot, he landed a mighty kick directly on the door's face.

The wooden surface held, but with a crashing sound, the entire door sprang open, away from them, and they bolted into the dark space just seconds before the wave began to crest fully and fall in the hall behind them.

Ŧ

"Where in Hell are we now?"

The door had slammed shut behind them, blocking most of the corridor's light.

"Another hall, I think," Ava replied. "It's a hallway in a house."

Nearly obscured by shadows, windows lined the walls – but whatever lay outside the large, many chambered house could not be seen.

Is it night out there?

Or is there something out there that makes the dark?

"This way!" she called, and now he, too, saw the immense stairway just ahead. Deeply fashioned in dark wood, it curved high, leading to the floors above and from at least that first landing – pale light came down.

There was no choice; water had begun to pool at their feet. From the closed door at their backs, a faint creaking was heard, low but growing louder. They took to their heels, taking the stairs two at once.

"How did Alice get out of this?" he gasped. They had halted on a landing, having raced many floors up. The stairs seemed endless, rising upward interminably, at least four or five levels higher than where they stood. Yet up was the only way out – from far below, the sound of slowly splintering wood reached them, and Ava panted out Carroll's solution as they ran upward.

"She swam – out of the lake of tears she herself had cried. That was after she changed size from huge to three inches tall. And I don't see that option here!"

She was right; below them, water was creeping up, slowly submerging the stairs one by one, landing by landing. A breach must have opened far below, the door might hold completely only moments more.

They flew upward level after level, nearly colliding with one another at the very top – for the stairs and stairwell ended abruptly at a blind landing – with no exit.

At least not one they could use. There, at the top of the landing, one wall held a large window.

It was a plain, ordinary window. One that might appear in any house you might happen to have, if you lived in a castle. The window was wide, but barred; heavy iron bars filled the frame, top to bottom. The space between those bars was less than a foot across – far too narrow to allow them escape.

"What now?" Cass cried, as he tried and failed to budge even one of the bars from the window's frame.

The Knight pulled her dagger. Fiercely she began to whittle away the wood that held the nearest bar in place. The blade tore away chunk after chunk of frame, but not enough to free the bar. She renewed her assault. Perspiration soon matted the red hair and the bar she worked on loosened in its place – but only that. He joined her at the window. They yanked at the bar, striking it, tearing at it, while it steadfastly resisted every effort to dislodge it from its place.

Then both drew back in horror – within the wall, the window – bars and all – had begun to move. A low slithering, groaning sound came from the area about the window as slowly but steadily the window rose higher and higher in the wall's surface. In moments it would be above their heads. In moments any hope of using the window as an exit would be lost.

Dark water now swirled in the stairwell less than a landing below them. The Knight turned to him, and shouted in desperation.

"Cass! Do something!"

Use what you have – or die.

It was there in his head – the Gryphon's words, its warning.

A strange calm descended over him. The Knave was filled with sudden need, an urge, potent, overwhelming. His mind went utterly blank; still without thinking, with only the vision of their struggling out their last moments, choking under water – he tore open the bag at his belt and thrust in his hand.

His hand came out – a card lay across his palm.

The Queen of Cups.

Ava stood motionless. She watched as the face of the young man at her side paled, and his eyes focused on something infinitely far in the distance. A light shone about him and Caspian Hythe spoke, and the Chevalière, with her hand still reaching for the bar that could not be freed, was silent, rapt.

The Joker's voice, low yet penetrating, was unlike anything she had ever heard before, as if it came from another time, another realm. The voice seemed everywhere at once, imperious, charged with a dark, terrible power. A chanting song, commanding and irresistible, came to stirring life in the stairwell.

> "*I call the West .....*
> *I call the West ...*
> *....of Cups – the Queen.*
> *Her heart unknown, Her face unseen.*
> *From the waters – UNDINE rise!*
> *Drownéd land, and nimbus skies.*
> *Mistress of the sea-washed sand,*
> *Hearken Ye at my command!*
> *Hear my Call! To All below!*
> *Stay the waters – halt the flow!*
> *I call... the West...."*

From deep below them, a low pounding came, as of the crashing of waves as they rolled over a beach, a beach infinitely distant, made of countless small stones, whose whisper rose up, even as the waves receded. Then, from those very depths, came something that stopped the breath of the girl with the dagger still in her hand.

It was a song, it could be little else, and it grew, echoing up from far down the drowned stairwell whose flights were now flooded with dark, deep emerald tides.

It rose from the water itself. There were words in the song, pure and sweet and ethereal, full of the story of water – of liquid rising and falling, of water dropping as rain, pattering from ice daggers as they melted into life giving streams, as rivulets that sparkled and rippled with the music of the earth itself.

And throughout the song streamed colour. Sapphire, royal blue, opal, the light- filled shades of every sea on earth were in the melody that rose, and Ava stared down at the water that now slowed in its ascent. The water's surface moved, for something was crawling up the flooded stairs, taking them one by one, as it made its way up through the water, drawing closer and closer to them.

Finally, she beheld it clearly – the creature with hair long and streaming, hair that floated about a face half maiden and half fish, a woman whose wide eyes were so nearly human, whose gills fluttered, opening and closing softly, in time with the tide that was heard and felt, yet was utterly unseen. Her body, nearly at the surface now, was clothed in sheer fabric that sparkled – or was it Her skin, covered with countless scales, minute and trembling, like scintillating sparks of rainbow- hued droplets catching a hidden moon's iridescent light?

The Undine's head reached and broke the water's surface. As Her form passed above it, and as She rose to stand, Her feet remained bathed in dark, flowing water, and words came to float in the air, even as Her hair lifted and swirled about the face of the Elemental.

Gazing at Her, Cass slowly went down upon his knees. The being looked down upon him. Like the faint, irresistible murmur of wind over water, Her speech echoed in the stairwell, even as his had done.

"*The West replies…*
The Key is played and turned and cast,
Its power fled while moments passed.
UNDINE risen! See them fall!
Fates of men, and waters – All!
Beware! The Woods hold golden eyes.

123

Sweetest tongue hides deadly size!
You have but single passage won,
The Card is played – the Key is gone!"

On his knees, the Joker turned Mage stared up at Her.

Beautiful, She was, pure as sunlight playing over the waves, powerful as the thundering surf that foams, disguising the deadly thrall of the seas on every shore. The card slipped from his shaking fingers – before it touched the waters curling about the Undine's feet, the paper had folded, and shriveled and vanished into a wisp of pale, verdant smoke.

The creature stepped forward.

Then She bent low, before the Mage. Drawing his face to Hers, She kissed the young man on his knees at Her feet.

She rose. Sea-green eyes now held those of the Knight. The Undine stepped back, away, down into waters that were slowly sinking, dissolving into them even as sand, freed from its earthly prison, explodes into wild, surging freedom in the welcoming surf.

124

Down, down the water sank, unveiling stair after stair, a waterfall in reverse – in moments it would be a trickle, soon it would utterly disappear, out of sight far below.

With his face and hair drenched with sweat, Cass rose unsteadily to his feet. A small line of blood showed at his nostril. Ava spoke his name.

He did not move.

He could not hear her.

To him, both the landing and the stairwell seemed to grow dim, darkening – what he saw and still heard in his mind was the sea, the soft, soothing sound of waves, of water eternal and irresistible – and a sweet song that lingered, inviting, alluring – urging him to come, to follow.

Blind to everything about him, oblivious to the girl at his side, his hand reached out, reached out longingly, hungrily, down – toward dark water that still swirled, receding below them. The Knight cried out. The Mage stumbled then, nearly losing his footing, lurching hard against the wall.

Suddenly he felt strong arms about him, gripping him tightly.

Holding him up by sheer force, steadying him, with legs spread wide to pinion him against the wall, Ava's hands were over him, on his chest, his face, touching his cheek, his lips, and she called his name, over, and over. When his vision finally cleared, her face was beside his, her eyes searching his.

He was still breathing hard but now he could see her clearly. She was close, her body pressed against his, her red hair blazing, her lips moist, parted. So close was she to him, that he was aware of her scent, full and sweet about him.

Full, and sweet – and human. Fitz.

"Hey. Welcome back," she murmured. Her hand rose to his forehead, pushing aside a lock of his wet hair.

She released him then. She watched the water as it drained away, stair by stair, taking with it the Undine's spell. Amazed, her hands dropped to her side – even as, from the window once more stationary and at eye level with their heads, the iron bar she had sought to free slid loose from its place and clattered to the floor at their feet.

Chapter 12

GOLDEN EYES

Who knew that Knights carried rope?

Such were the Knave's thoughts; for one terrifying second, he straddled the open air. Then, steadying himself, his boots landed hard against stone, and he started down the moss- slick outer walls of the castle.

For castle it was, when clearly seen from the outside, but a castle odd in the extreme.

The memory of the Undine's call was fading; he'd had no chance to dwell upon what he himself had felt, in his mind, in his body – when the Knight had touched him, striving to release him from the Elemental's potent sorcery.

For after seeing him safe and steady on his feet, Ava had immediately reached into the bag at her own belt. Out of this had come a surprising expanse of silken grey rope. Narrow, ghostly pale it seemed in the diffuse light that permeated the space from the window. It had been easy to hoist themselves up to the window, where one end of the rope was tied to an iron bar. The other end was passed around the Knight, and out the window she had gone. She soon disappeared, rappelling hand over hand, down the outside wall.

Ava stood now, steadying the rope – on ground that should have been far below – but wasn't.

"It's not what you think!" That had been her shout as she had worked her way downward, and once he had struggled through the aperture and started down the wall, he had stopped only twice, mystified.

Racing the tide of rising water, they had bounded up at least eight flights of stairs, of that he was certain. That should have left them many storeys above the ground floor.

In any other world.

Not so in this one.

Cass was perched on the castle's side – he looked up at the window through which he had just passed, a window that never appeared more than two stories above the ground.

Not possible.

Except here, of course.

Many confounded looks led to the same baffling conclusion – the space inside the castle was greater than its outer dimensions suggested. He wondered now what lay in the many rooms that they had seen in their headlong flight upstairs. Yet, even greater astonishment met him when he finally jumped down to join the Knight.

She was staring up at the dark edifice, and when he looked up, he, too, gaped.

The distance from where they stood to the window high above was well over forty meters – a distance many, many times greater than what it had seemed in their spider-like crawl down the castle's side.

Is all space here obeying a different set of laws? If it does – where is the user's guide?

The rope still dangled from the bar in the window frame. A moment later, all along its length, that rope began to glow, and in seconds – had begun to smoke. Before their eyes, the rope burned away completely. A light rain of pale grey ash sifted down onto the grass at their feet, grass whose surface began to shimmer, as if lit by bright starlight.

They leapt backward; the turf now glowed silver, almost white hot with heat that could only be imagined.

The next instant, curling and growing from out of the ashes scattered on the turf, a new rope began to steadily take form.

When the rope's writhing and twisting finally ceased, Ava reached down and retrieved the thing from where it lay, neatly coiled in the cool grass. Cool, also was the rope to the touch and, as puzzled as was Cass, Ava tucked it back inside her leather bag. She looked up to the window high above.

"Do you suppose the bar has grown back into place, too?" she wondered.

"I hope not," he replied. "I don't see a door on this side."

It was true. At the ground level, no apparent access to the building could be found. They stood on a narrow lawn under a pearl grey sky shot with golden light. Tall stands of yews closely hugged many of the castle's visible sides. Beyond the lawn, lines of trees, yews and pines, tall and old and hung with moss, spread outward, forming a veritable hedge about the enigmatic structure.

The Knight's hand tensed on her sword pommel.

"Look," she breathed. "Look up there."

From the window they had just left, a form had appeared. Both the Knight and the Knave drew back – for an eerie call floated down to them from the heights.

It was answered – by furtive movement in the yews directly across from them.

"Who – is that?" Ava said.

"You mean – what is that?"

An astounding change came over the young woman at his side. Infused with sudden, raw strength and power, her entire form tensed. With resolute face and her body in battle stance, she shoved the Knave back, away from the looming grey stones that seemed suddenly no longer empty, but rather menacingly alive.

"Time to go," she cried.

"Where?"

"Into the woods."

"Like that's better? We've been warned," he said.

"We have no choice! I want something solid at my back; I want it now! I want the safety of the trees," she exclaimed.

One more look at the yews – then they turned and fled.

For eyes – golden, bright and infinitely terrifying – now glared out from the tree boughs, not forty paces away. The two ran like the wind; there was no time to look back, no chance to see that the one at the window no longer watched, no way to know that the eyes in the greenery had winked out, vanishing as suddenly as they had first appeared.

There was more. Had they remained behind, they would have seen the high, oaken door that appeared from nowhere, as it grew into shape from out of the very stones of the castle's wall. They would have seen that door, grating softly, slowly open – allowing a single shadowy figure to pass through, a figure that would follow in their footsteps as they ran on, desperate to reach the safety of the trees.

The safety of the trees....

Ŧ

At first the man had walked, then run, pushing his way forward, desperate to find a way through the pine glade.

He was weary; slowed by his fear, checked by the heavy task of forcing his way through thorns and brambles that clutched at his robes, seemingly bent on stopping him. Now all he could manage was a halting stumble.

In the midst of the smallest of clearings, he came to a breathless halt. The soft carpet of dried needles muffled his footfalls. Close, so close; the pines, tall and dense, threateningly pressed around him. This was old forest; little light penetrated here. Yet, there was just enough to reflect off the gems that adorned the fingers of both his trembling hands, and the jewels woven into his courtly robes.

She warned me. That she did; not to try the Wood – not now. Oh, my Duchess! Who will protect you, now? Yet, if I may but reach them; if I may only warn them.

If I may but reach them in time.

The Duke's shaking hand rose to his cheek where the thorns had cut his face. His fingers came away wet with blood.

His breeches were spattered with mud, disheveled, and a great tear could be seen in one of his tunic's sleeves. From his fine, plumed cap, he pulled off and picked out the few creepers that had nearly torn it from him in his flight. The cap was replaced with stolid determination, back upon his head.

All will be set right! Yet how I wish I had held my tongue!

Another deep breath, he was ready to go on. But, no – something was amiss.

His heart began to pound again – the snap of a twig – slight but tangible, had come from just behind, where the rough path he had followed melted into shadow.

Now it was quiet, so quiet. A great menacing stillness seemed to descend from the trees about him. Paralyzed with fear, he peered anxiously about him, praying to see past the shadows that seemed to rise up around him. He stumbled back, shrinking away from the strange fingers of dark that seemed to creep out from the very ground beneath the towering trees, reaching for him.

The Duke's fearful gasp caught in his throat; He dare not move now, perhaps if he were as still as he could be…

He cried out softly.

It was too late. Now he saw them, there – up in the trees.

Now there was no doubt – they saw him.

The eyes!

Yellow eyes, golden eyes; eyes that grew brighter with each passing second, with each beat of the heart hammering in his heaving chest. The eyes grew ever more brilliant, nearer and nearer – and now larger and larger until they loomed, aflame with wrath – from the tree limb directly over his head.

His scream was loud and long.

It rang throughout the trees. It was heard by a Knight and a Knave, who raced forward under the towering pines, following the fading echo of a dying man's last, hopeless call for help.

It was too late. When they reached the smallest of clearings, all that they found was the lifeless form of a man's torn body, sprawled upon the ground.

Dead eyes stared upward in horror. The gems on its hands and robes had lost their brilliance, eclipsed by the blood that streamed freely from the savagely torn throat.

Chapter 13

SIZE DOES MATTER

I feel naked without it now.

Seated cross-legged on the ground, Ava studied her sword, with its bright point driven deep into the turf, still surprised at her growing pleasure in merely regarding the bare blade.

I – who have never before held a weapon much less used one – what else will change the longer we remain here?

And what of the Knave?

Her eyes were now on Cass who was carefully examining the body on the forest floor. He rose to his feet, then circled the Duke's remains, coolly studying the bloody clothes and gaping wounds from every angle.

Sword, dagger, rope, and more; these weapons are mine.

Is his the power, the power of will that may keep us alive?

The Joker – the Knave that rises, to become the Mage....the Sorcerer.

There was little to see in the tree -ringed periphery of the clearing. Yet the sense of being not just closely observed, but keenly evaluated – that did not leave her. This she had felt since they had arrived at the scene of slaughter. The trees were ominous and dark, with gnarled limbs twisting oppressively down around them. Yet from above, a soft glow marked a clear broad sliver of sky.

Is it dawn?

Or just the dark, fleeing from something stronger, more powerful? For the dark – here – is very strong.

And death walks here unchallenged.

They had found the scattered tracks even before they had discovered the body. Something monstrous had tread here, tread heavily, the sheer size of the tracks was stunning. Signs were all about on the soft ground where pine needles had been pushed aside. The Knave looked up from his grim task.

He came to her. He, too, marked the light in the sky. Then he sat, wiping a thin smear of blood from his hand onto the dry forest floor.

"Did you see his throat? Whatever killed himwas larger than a cougar; much larger. Something pretty vicious has been at work here, Fitz."

"It's not finished yet. There's something; something is still here – in the Wood. Do you feel it?"

No sign, nor sound of any birds, so little sound anywhere; the silence was remarkable – watchful. He nodded. At their feet was a chaos of clothes and flesh, ripped and crumpled. Whatever had done this had found supreme pleasure in the act itself. They moved closer to the trees.

"The rings on his hands," said Cass. "The ensigns, his tunic with its crest – he's royal. A Count?"

"A Duke."

He shook his head. "I don't remember a Duke being in the story."

"There isn't one."

"Maybe this is what took him out of it. But what the hell was he doing out here? There was a Duchess. If he's the Duke, Fitz — where is the Duchess?"

The Knight replied softly. "Maybe she had the sense to stay home."

"Of course she did," came the voice.

Both humans leapt up and looked wildly about them. They had entered under the pines. The Knight pulled both sword and dagger.

Cass ignored his own short blade –for the first time, without even realising it – he put his hand full on the wand at his belt.

From the dark tree limbs over their heads, the voice came again. Its richness – soothing and placating, as redolent and murderous as poisoned honey– could not disguise the vicious lie just beneath.

"He *would* be the foolish one, of course," the voice continued. "If *you* were more wise than politic, you'd agree – he was *mad* to try the Wood now; quite mad. I do so hope that you are not mad, too."

"We are not mad. But where are you?" Cass enquired warily.

"Knowing that will not save you," came the low reply.

"Shall we see about that?"

"I don't think so. I don't believe *you* see anything *at all*."

Cass did not reply, for the feeling of deadly threat was suddenly overpowering and with it, from deep within him, it had come again –the sensation of need, insistent and potent, unaccompanied by conscious intent.

Warmth, full and palpable; it surged through him, growing more and more intense, irresistible. The hand resting upon the wand throbbed, the weapon itself grew warm, thickening and pulsing under his hand. Unable to disobey the compulsion to act, Cass' hand closed over the wand, which moved of its own accord, settling itself against his palm.

The will of man – in union with the divine – brings knowledge – and power.

The Knave freed the wand from his belt – and raised it.

Etched brightly against the dark carven ivory, the runes encircling its tip grew startlingly clearer. The wand itself moved in his grasp and its tip flamed with sudden light that spread, surrounding the young Mage, etching the pine needles and tree limbs until they stood out in a patchwork of near-blinding brilliance set off by pitch- dark shadow. Light spilled out until finally, on the tree limb above and across from them, the speaker was revealed.

Ava looked at the thing revealed in the tree. She cast a quick look again at Cass.

First had come an eerie look into his eyes, as if there were something in the distance only the Mage could see. As if upon an unheard signal, the man's hand had then closed over the wand – to Ava, not one, but many hands, each glowing from within lay across the wand, and then light had come – flooding out, surrounding them. The Knight tore her eyes from the Mage – she, too, gazed up, up into the tree, where something inhuman, and blood thirsty – gazed down upon them, its orbs full of shifting, cursed, yellow vehemence.

"Golden eyes," she whispered. "Cass, don't move."

Before he could respond, Ava had left him. She walked boldly to the tree and there addressed the creature that lay stretched across the wide bough, a creature that only appeared to be a Cat.

"I wondered when we would actually *see* you," said the Knight.

A loud, resonant purr floated down.

"Oh, I hadn't left. I am always here. I am everywhere – that is the command, the rule. You could have seen me at any time. But, it's really all about that, isn't it? *Seeing*; seeing *clearly*, the difference between what you believe is true and what is true in actuality; realizing that this difference can be a wide one. Then, it's about finding the strength – and faith – to reconcile the two. I am at your service, Chevalière. You *will* let me know, won't you – if I may help you in the slightest way?" the Cat offered in the sweetest tones imaginable.

"I shall be certain to take that – upon advisement."

The creature rose slowly to its feet and stretched languorously. Far too large for a cat, its striped and spotted fur was lustrously thick; the wide golden eyes set in a head whose span exceeded that of a fair-sized dog. The Knight's gloved hand tightened on her sword hilt – for when the Cat rose, its form seemed somehow indistinct for a second, and its golden eyes narrowed. The creature was positively grinning down at them – revealing a full maw of savagely sharp teeth.

"You did well in the house, I was surprised. *She* was surprised, too. I was wondrously amused," it said, in syllables of sugared acid.

"We are delighted to have amused you. And where is She now?" asked the Knight.

The Cat yawned artlessly.

"At the end of the path, of course. You'll get there; all in good time. Yet, I'm *thrilled* to tell you croquet will not be the game of the day! No, indeed! There are finer games than that to play, aren't there? Just ask your Mage; *he* knows, doesn't he? How quickly he learns! How skillfully he perfects his – craft, shall we say? A craft at odds with yours, I might add. I wonder how long it will take before… but I digress. Games, always games, even as She plays! I do so hope that I may play one with *you*, myself."

"Play one with me. Like the last game you played – the one just beyond in the clearing," Cass said softly.

The creature's eyes fastened on the Mage. Long and searchingly, the thing took him in, from head to foot. The Cat's golden eyes narrowed again – evil was in them, pure, unhallowed, and unhampered by conscience, evil and more, for here was a gaze exuberant with the creature's need to kill, to kill slowly, painfully, fearsomely. Its voice altered, now deeper, guttural and grating, akin to a parody of a human voice.

"You, too, shall play. We shall see how well your judgment serves you. I wonder – how shall your Lady like the games you will learn to play here with her – at the end? Will she be yet alive to experience them – *in all their passion* – in their full pleasure? In all their marvelous terror?"

The Mage tensed, for suddenly, the creature's voice rang only in his mind.

Have you come to see, Mage?

Have you seen your end, for the time is not long – and have you seen hers – at your hand?

The beast once more spoke aloud. "But, we are wasting time. I'll come down – let me show you how to play," growled the Cat.

The Cat gracefully dropped down to a closer limb – and, as it moved, its form shifted, its size changing before their eyes.

Fully twice as large as before, the Cat was leopard-like, and its inch long talons scored deeply into the tree's bark as it crouched, tensing.

But the Mage stepped forward, putting himself between Ava and the thing in the tree. Intensely bright, a beam of light billowed out from the wand's tip. The Cat winced and drew back, blinking hard. Flattened against the limb, there it clung, its tail lashing furiously from side to side. Its eyes were now flaming, malevolent, their pupils enormous as it regarded the motionless young man.

"You'll stay where you are – and as you are," said the Mage.

"Is that your *Command?*" the beast asked eagerly, its voice rich with suppressed excitement and for no reason she could name – the Knight felt fear.

"It is my *wish*," the Mage responded, but he did not lower his weapon and light pulsed angrily before the Cat's face. Its head lowered – as it did so, the wand's light receded, dimming to a soft glow. With a loud purr, the beast collected itself, settling down on the limb. With a horrible laugh, it sheathed its claws and smiled at them.

"Then I shall do as you *wish; for now*," the creature added. "So! Advance – if you can! I trust that before we meet again, you will learn *faster* what to do and *how*. I should say – I can guarantee, that *She* does not equal me in *politeness*. But don't you want to see *him?*"

"We do," replied Ava. "Where is he?"

The Cat yawned lazily, its long teeth white in the gloom.

"Who can say? Or rather, who will? No matter. All paths lead to Her, and from Her – to him." Its huge head turned from one side of the Wood, then the other. "I will tell you this – *that* way takes you to the Duchess. And *that* way – to the house of the March Hare. But he really *is* mad, so you will take care, won't you? I do *so* want you alive – for a little bit longer."

Slowly, as if it were leaving a fight that any alley cat had just lost, the thing turned on the limb – and in just doing so, its size transformed once more. Nearly as large as a tiger, it gazed down at them with enormous golden eyes. Those eyes stayed on the Knight for a moment. But its regard stayed longest on the Mage and its eyes narrowed malevolently

147

before it turned aside. The gigantic thing padded away, slipping silently into the shadows at the end of the bough, and the light from Cass' wand ebbed away. They did not see the Cat actually vanish; rather it seemed swallowed up in the dappling of light and dark in the mosaic of the tree's own needles.

Ava sheathed her sword; her dagger stayed out and her finger ran pensively along the weapon's blade.

"How do you know he won't come back?" Cass wondered.

"He will. But not yet," answered the Knight.

What made you decide to use the wand?"

He paused. "I didn't. It came to me somehow. In the castle, did you actually know there was rope in your bag?"

He turned away, gazing once more into the trees, and then back at the wand he carried, so close to his body.

The Knight shook her head.

"At the window, all I wanted was to get out – to get down." She looked suddenly again at the

Knave, earnestly searching his face; he could never have imagined why.

He had taken up the wand and invoked its power, and she had seen something inexplicable. Not only had light streamed from the wand's tip – a strange light had also played over the features of the man. Once he had assumed the role of Mage, soft, ephemeral, pale and blue – a symbol had been etched brightly against his skin. Unfathomable but certain, it had lasted but a second; now, however, the Knight's thoughts ran deep.

A sign – a sign of what?

This time – he was not weakened by the invocation. Does the Wand grant protection?

Or has the Mage ascended and reached the next level?

Cass returned to the body. He knelt close beside it. Gently, the Joker covered the man with the tattered remnants of his own cloak. He paused, considering – then he carefully removed the dead nobleman's ensign ring from the bloody hand, pocketing it. Swiftly, the sky above was lightening – there, against the sky, he caught a glimpse – of dark wings. He leapt to his feet and eyes up, raced after.

Calling, the Knight followed him, catching him in a smaller clearing where he stood, eyes still on the heavens.

"Wings," he whispered. "I saw wings – something in the sky."

Ava craned her eyes upward; there was nothing but the thin clouds and haze and the eerie golden light.

"The Gryphon," she said.

"No! No, it was a hawk – *the hawk* – from the upper world."

She frowned. "Are you certain?"

"I am."

"But, Cass, how is it possible?"

He smiled weakly. "We're here, aren't we?"

Ava studied the clearing, with its ring of trees, its shadows still dark in the middle of day.

"What else can cross here – from above?" she asked.

"What else can travel back?" he muttered – as the sound of horns, wildly blown, reached them from the forest depths – drawing closer and closer. They sought cover in a dense thicket and the Knight spoke low and hoarsely.

"This is not in the book – but whoever it is, I don't want to meet them yet! I say we go, now – to the Duchess."

He followed her; she led them from the thicket and they ran through the woods, ever further from the sound of horns until, after some distance, the trees began to thin. Leaving the forest, they moved guardedly into country that seemed to have felt the hand of man. The pine glades were at their back; stony hills and rolling country was before them – that, and more.

Sheltered among landscaped gardens, fountains and broad lawns, a large, stately house loomed in the near distance. The Knight and the Knave drew closer; above the massive door, the lintel bore the same arms as those they had seen on the tunic of the murdered Duke.

They were not alone in seeking out the Duchess.

The grounds were crowded with scores of men. Dark clad soldiers, squads of them, masked and armed, roamed the ancient cobbled avenue that led to the house.

Into and out of that house the soldiers passed, and upon their tunics, gloves and all of their weapons – were the jet-black ensigns of the Queen of Hearts.

Chapter 14

DECLARO

"You there! Halt!"

He stood barely a hundred paces away and his face turned directly toward them the moment they stepped from the cover of the trees.

Indisputably, he was the Captain – with his team of Guards arrayed around him, he and his men raced toward Cass and Ava.

Those two found themselves surrounded; there was no question of movement or escape. They remained where they stood, silent and helpless within a ring of bright blades and glittering spear points.

Cass' hand rested on the hilt of his wand. The Knight made no move to arm herself; rather, she waited until the Captain was near. Then to Cass' surprise, she went down on one knee. There she remained, with bowed head, directly before the man.

He was very tall; his face, alone among his men was bare, and sternly he regarded the Knight at his feet. Then he regarded the equally tall young man beside her – one who did not kneel in the presence of the Captain of the Black Queen's High Guard.

"Rise, Knight," he said at last and Ava stood, touching her hand to her sword and her shoulder in token.

"My Thane," she began. "Your pardon for coming upon you without warning. We seek the Duchess." Her words had apparently forestalled his question for the Thane's expression was now one of cool suspicion.

"Pardon is granted. To what purpose do you seek my Lady? You do not come to seek the Duke?" he asked.

"No, Sir. The Duke is dead," she replied.

The Thane's eyes widened; he frowned.

"We came at his call – we were too late. You will find him in the pine glade," said Cass.

The Captain advanced until he stood eye to eye with Cass; a long moment passed.

"In the *Wood?*" How came he there?"

"We bring *word* of the Duchess' loss – not explanations," the Knave replied.

The Black Queen's Captain studied the young man, a young man whose gaze remained as steady, as fixed as did his own. He turned to the Knight.

"I see. The Duke is dead – and you have no explanations. You seek the Duchess. That Lady is expecting you?"

Cass saw Ava stiffen, but at that moment, the Duchess herself appeared in the wide doorway of the house. Before any could speak further, she called out and hurried to meet them.

"At last! You are here – I knew you would come!" she cried. "Captain thank you for finding my guests. May they come inside and be refreshed?"

Warily, he observed the three arrayed before him; his eyes stayed fixed on the Duchess as he spoke.

"The Duke is dead, my Lady."

The Duchess stared at him. Her hair was long and blonde, coiled elegantly about her face and she wore no headdress. The Lady's full, fair features and ruddy cheeks blanched at the Captain's words. Cass watched as she struggled to speak, and for a second, he thought he saw tears in the pale blue eyes.

"Dead? Dead. My Lord is dead. Alas. Alas for us all," said the Duchess, sadly. "He was a rash man. But how did this happen? May I see him?"

No, there are no tears, it's a trick of the light.

She speaks only to the Thane, her eyes never leave him. It's as though Fitz and I aren't even here.

Did she know the Duke was dead before he told her?

The Thane made no answer. His eyes stayed on the Duchess, who murmured something low, returning his gaze with a sweet mildness that made the Joker wonder. Cass stole a look at Ava. Her eyes were also on the Duchess, taking in the woman's stately form, her immaculate attire of silks and satin, and bright jewels.

The Duchess fell silent; unexpectedly, the Thane bowed to the Lady.

"Madame, allow us to attend the Duke. You have had heavy news this day. We will leave you here with your friends."

He turned on his heel. Followed by his men, he crossed the lawns, and passed from sight beneath the dark, overhanging boughs of the trees. The

Duchess watched them leave, then sighed mightily. She turned to Cass and Ava.

"Will you come?"

Ŧ

"It is never easy; especially now!

The last few years – I could tell you volumes! One never knows whom one may trust – or not. But you are here now, as has been our hope, our dearest wish, and soon we shall see what will come."

The Duchess smiled at them. Her servant removed their empty plates and goblets; he crossed to the heavy doors at the end of the great salon, closing them behind him. The meal had been a marvel, yet the Knave sat restless and disturbed.

Nothing is as it should be.

Far from it.

From his seat on the low, deeply cushioned divan, he again considered the room, with its rich furnishings, vaulting and elegant ceilings. The sunlight that flooded in from the high windows warmed neither the room's splendid trappings, nor him.

Across from him, on the fine settee, Ava sat calmly at the Duchess' side. The Knight had removed one of her gloves during the meal; it lay across her knee. Her other hand – the sword hand – remained gloved and rested close to the pommel of the girl's sheathed weapon as she spoke.

"How fortunate is Your Grace to have the particular favour of Her Majesty's own Thane at need."

The Duchess lowered her eyes. She rose and walked to the windows. Her hand came up; the brightness was prodigious, and she drew the curtains to stem the tide of light.

"My loyalties are now as they have ever been – incontestable," she replied.

"Of course," Ava remarked. "I was not speaking of loyalty. Was it not only on our arrival that your Grace learned of the Duke's loss? Why then was the Thane here, and with such a force of men? Were you in danger?"

As she gazed at the Knight, the look in the Duchess' eyes was unaccountable. She did not rejoin them at their seats before the wide fireplace. Instead, from the sideboard, she poured wine and remained there, as she swirled it in her goblet, then tasted it. Returning to the settee, she placed the goblet on the low table at Cass' side. Then she sat beside the Knight.

"You have a kind soul. I'm touched at your solicitude, my dear," said the Duchess. "It was I who asked the noble Guards to come here; the Duke had not yet returned, I gave in to my fear. Fear can be a mighty motivator. One can never have too much assurance, too much purchase – can one? Surely you agree? I see that you, yourself, do not travel alone."

The Lady looked directly at Cass and he frowned; her regard was deeply scrutinising as she addressed him.

"Of course, I had word of the Knight's progress," said the Duchess. "Doubtless, the Knight would be traveling in company – yet, I confess, I was surprised to see *you*, my good Knave, pleasantly surprised, of course. Tell me – have you a consort? Or do you attend the Knight – as such?"

Silence descended in the room. Colour rose briefly into Ava's cheeks; her companion betrayed none of the emotion he himself felt at the unexpected use of this word – and its implication.

The Lady seemed to perceive what was in his mind for her regard passed from cool assessment to something quite different. Her eyes took in her tall guest, from his shoulders, to his powerful hands, to the long limbs grown strong. Under that close gaze, as if the woman herself might have touched him – Cass felt warmth spreading through him, warmth that rose to his lips – but he did not smile.

"As you said, Your Grace; one can never have too much assurance. I am here as many things. And who can say what *any* of us might become."

"Who can say, indeed?" the Duchess agreed. "What can be said is this: that you – Joker, Knave, whatever else you may be – seem to have started down a dangerous path – with or without the Knight."

Cass' eyes stayed on her. "I stay or leave at the Knight's pleasure," he said softly.

A smile touched the Lady's lips.

"At the Knight's pleasure! Her pleasure, indeed. And you—who are here as many things – who wonders what any of us might become – companion, consort – conqueror, perhaps? Land, treasure, even fear – those are simple things, easy to hold in check, easy to control – *yet, whatever shall we do with those whom we conquer?* You stay or leave at her pleasure, you say, yet I think you will find the 'leaving' a far different matter than the 'staying'. But how lucky we are, right now. How lucky for us all, that you are here! And especially – how lucky is our Knight! Perhaps the time for sorrow is passing."

Her bright eyes had turned to Ava, whose cheeks no longer coloured, and whose gaze, shining and steady, did not drop under that penetrating regard.

Cass eyed their hostess steadily.

"Yet, we shared that sorrow, Madam. He must have been a good man. We would have liked to have known the Duke. What can you tell us of him?" he asked.

That Lady studied the rings on her fingers; and she seemed lost in her own thoughts for a moment.

"I cannot say. Some will miss him; some will shed tears. Shall I shed tears, too? If not for him; what of myself? Will there be time enough for tears? Shall it be in this life? The things that draw our tears

161

– and the things that do not – these are the things that show what we are. *She* never cries, you know," she added.

"She?" Ava asked.

"The Queen."

"Never?"

The Duchess looked at her.

"Why should she?" she replied.

The Knight frowned. "Surely everyone has known some occasion that merits an acknowledgment of loss – and what of error? Surely everyone has *done* something that … "

The Duchess smoothly cut her off.

"Everyone? A Queen is not just 'everyone'. We should not judge too harshly, I think, nor too hastily. Who may do so? Who is fit to do so? How can one fairly judge a Queen? *Power is all.* Yet I ask you – can one be condemned for doing what comes naturally? Should one be judged for reigning as one must?"

Cass regarded her closely. "Those arguments have long been the proven rhetoric of tyrants, Lady."

The Lady smiled again. "Come, now. We are none of us children in this, neither the Knight nor you yourself; I think I make myself understood. Are there not other subjects more fitting to the occasion of your visit? Wouldn't you like to know where *he* is?"

Unexpected, it was, so unexpected that Cass and Ava were stunned. The Duchess laughed gaily.

"*The Hatter.* Of course, I meant the Hatter! But, you knew that, already – as well as the way, didn't you? You must go on or you must go back. There's no riddle, at least not there. Games, always games – wise are those who have the sense to see – and to profit by them. *'Will you, won't you? Will you, won't you – come and join the dance?'* For it is like a dance, is it not, this life, this game? It is always our choices – when do we play – and with whom. Is that a partner you see before you – or an adversary? Can you tell, young Knave? Are you wise enough yet?"

Ava drew back in her seat and stared at the elegant woman beside her.

She never says 'her Majesty.'
She always says 'the Queen'.

Mind racing, she exhaled sharply and Ava now cast an urgent look at Cass. But sitting erect and stiff in his seat, the Joker was no longer following the conversation.

He was transfixed – his eyes riveted on the goblet on the table beside him, from the surface of whose wine a thin wisp of cold mist had suddenly begun to curl.

The silence in the room was now all encompassing, profound.

The Duchess sat forward. Her eyes were on the Knight and a single word escaped her, low and indistinguishable. Yet it was enough, for the Knight immediately looked back – directly into the Lady's eyes, those mild, blue eyes in that sweet face. The girl did not look away but slowly she removed her glove from her sword hand; she remained still, with the glove clutched in her fist.

The Duchess' hand rose. Her fingers closed tightly on Ava's arm, yet the girl's eyes remained locked to those of their hostess. The Duchess drew the girl closer, so close that now their faces nearly touched – the Knight made no effort to free herself.

The Mage's heart was pounding in his chest.

Cass rose to his feet. He looked down on the Duchess, but his words were directed at the one who sat, like a bird frozen before a snake, unmoving, barely breathing, at her side.

"Ava. Look at me."

The Knight made no response.

"Ava. Don't look at her – look at me," he repeated.

The Duchess never took her eyes from the Knight and her lips moved, wordlessly. Then she whispered aloud. "Come child, we don't need to trouble ourselves with him, do we?"

"*Fitz* – look at me, I said," urged the Knave. "*Do it, do it now.* Look *only* at me."

The girl did not hear him. Motionless she remained and a smile spread across the Duchess' face; Cass' heart sank.

She cannot hear you.

She is not able to hear you.

Use what you have – or die.

Unconsciously, he took a deep breath and held it, and the room dimmed around him.

Then, like a torrent released, into his mind surged a veritable flood – of words, sounds, symbols. For the space of several moments, he was helpless, reeling, blinded by the tide of word after word, as image after image materialised, looming into recognition. From a murmur, the words grew to a litany – harsh, guttural, the rough tongue of a language dead for a thousand years or more.

Panting now, with his breath coming hard, fast and deep, keenly and without warning, his entire body seemed to come alive.

Forcibly it came, just as it had in the stairwell – the wave, spreading upward like flame. The searing warmth widened, spilling across his thighs, embracing his loins and rising upward, until it surged across his chest.

Throughout his frame, ardent sensation now flowed like a burning, exhilarating tide. It was no longer the Knave, but the Mage, the Sorcerer, whose bare hand stretched forth, reaching out toward the girl, and the air glittered and rippled about the naked, glowing flesh.

Every thought had been driven from his mind. All that remained was ordinance – to speak, to utter precisely what was now invocation. Little more than a whisper, yet his voice seemed to overpower the stillness of the room, a room suddenly grown dark and cold.

"My Knight – I Command Thee."

A shock ran through the girl's frame. Her face flushed; she gave a low, inarticulate cry.

Ava shuddered; then she sighed deeply and her head tipped back. For several seconds, the young woman's eyelids fluttered deliriously, then closed, as though she were lost, surrendered to a passion consuming, irresistible, felt, not seen. Her eyes opened again; her face turned, her eyes moved away from the piercing gaze of the one beside her – and the Chevalière looked up, directly into the eyes of the Mage.

There her gaze stayed.

The Knight wrenched her arm from the Duchess' grip and her free hand rose up, reaching, toward the Sorcerer. She struggled up, onto her feet; stumbling, she turned, backing away, away from the one on the couch. When she reached the Mage's side, he pulled her roughly behind him; then he spoke coldly to the Duchess.

"A game, you say? Indeed; it is quite the game, Lady – either one of words, or one of shadows. *Yet all must play.* Listen well. We are finished here – we are leaving now. You will not hinder her. You will not hinder *me*. We seek the Hatter; we will find him – you may rely upon it. And *you* may make riddles, as you please!"

Outside, the sun had fled. The wide room with its grand furnishings, its air heavy and still, seemed crowded with the coming, eager dark.

But the Duchess' eyes were like two pinpoints of frigid light. She rose slowly to her feet. Her voice was soft yet chilling in the vast chamber.

"I do indeed rely upon it, young Joker – young Knave – young *Mage*. You grow more interesting with each trial – how far you have come since that first night. Do you remember? You desired to get away from me. See where you ended – on the floor, on your hands and knees. I will see you there again, my Sorcerer – at my feet, with desires of an entirely different kind."

"I think not," came the Sorcerer's low reply.

"You have no choice – I rule here," said the Duchess.

"Do you? Do you *really?*"

For a moment, she was silent. It was the ravenous silence of a killing frost, the fiery silence of ice as it chokes away the life in its grip.

"Remember this, as you seek your Hatter –
especially with regards to your Knight – *remember
the fate of the Duke – and there are worse ways to
die, my dear Mage – worse by far.* As for riddles –
have you heard this one?"

"Said the Queen to the 'Knave',
Be you ever so brave –
Fail you must, if you try,
You will never get through.
Try your best; it's no matter.
Go – ask 'Mr. Hatter'!
He'll tell you, quite, sadly –
How much you can't do!"

As shadows streamed forward, driving before
them the light shrinking from the rooms, Caspian
Hythe stood motionless before her

His voice rose, echoing as had hers in the
room.

"Said the 'Knave' to the Queen—
Here I am – unforeseen!
This is not like before,

You are wasting your breath.
Let the Queen's tears stay hidden,
Soon forced – they'll be bidden.
Who walks in Her garden?
Who waits there – for Death?"

This time the Duchess' face went white – for the first time, uncertainty, nay, fear itself was in her eyes.

She quickly recovered. With her jaw set, she walked forward until she stood directly before Cass, who, still unmoving, returned her gaze. There they stood, face to face, the woman of glacial beauty, with eyes like cold blue flint – and the young man, as icy, as unflinching – as was she.

The Mage did not look away from his opponent – but his breath deepened.

"My Lord – can you hear me?" whispered the Knight, watching in growing horror as sparks of bitter light began to dance in the Duchess' eyes.

Desire – she desires him.

No – She covets him, as she might covet a new toy, a bright, new jewel for her hand.

As night covets the light of dawn.

The Mage exhaled; an eerie smile played over his lips.

"My Knight – *go*," he urged.

Ava backed away then ran from the room. Only when she had passed safely through the doors did the Sorcerer step back, away from the Duchess. He made a mocking reverence, the slightest nod of his head to the Lady, and followed the Knight.

Coldly, greedily, the Duchess watched him, taking in every aspect of his form, until the heavy front door clicked shut behind him.

She turned away. Calmly, she began to cross the room, toward the mansion's heart, where the fine, sturdy doors led to the wide staircase.

With each step she took, she was less and less alone in the vast and beautiful chamber.

For, as she walked – gliding in at the edge of sight, almost imperceptibly – long, sinuous fingers of darkness crept across the polished floors.

Pursuing her, as timid children might crawl after a harsh mistress, shadows followed the Duchess, dancing and playing soundlessly about her very heels as she passed.

She halted at the foot of the stairs; then started up, and with each stair, with each step upward – the form of the woman began to change. Her rich, bright robes seemed to dissolve, layer by layer, floating away as a pale but living mist. They grew more and more transparent with each moment, as the dew of gossamer spider webs vanishes in the cleansing light of dawn, dissolving to reveal the hidden snare beneath.

New and strikingly different now was the dress of the woman ascending the stairs.

Bold, resplendent and black was the raiment that now garbed the Lady, whose very face had altered even as had her clothes. High and lofty was the forehead, and ivory her cheeks, and her lips were curved in a smile, hard and crimson and cruel.

The eyes of the Duchess were mild and blue no longer – large, brilliant and dark they had become. As hard and cold as obsidian were the orbs in the Dark Lady's regal face as she paused on the landing at the top of the stairs where, from the darkest end of the long corridor, came a furtive rustling – and blood-red eyes shone out of the gloom. She reached the first door on the landing. She opened it and passed through.

A fire glowed weakly in the grate beyond, but the room was in shadow, as was now all the house.

With a Guard armed, and garbed and masked in ebony at her back, a woman sat in this room, in one of her own tall chairs. Her hands were tied behind her, and her fair mouth was bound tightly with black silk.

From her seat, the Duchess glared up at the woman who had come through the door, at the one who, tall and commanding, spoke, yet whose voice, while rich and sweet, was wintry, empty – utterly devoid of human spirit, benevolence, or mercy.

"Release her," said the Black Queen to her Guard.

The Guard freed the Duchess from her bonds and the owner of this house chafed her bruised wrists, and with blue eyes alive with anger, she rose to face her Liege.

"Where are they? What have you done to them?" demanded the Duchess.

A short wave from the Queen sent the Guard from the room.

"'To' them? My dear Duchess, why ever would I do anything '*to* them'?" replied the Black Queen. "But where are your manners, do I not at least merit a courtesy?"

The Duchess strode angrily about the room.

"After being attacked, bound and held prisoner in my own home – without even the subterfuge of a warrant – for what possible reason would I give Your Highness any such consideration?"

"Why, for saving your life, my dear," the Queen replied. "Now, now – I fully understand how you must feel. Please, believe me; it was necessary, for your own good, your own safety."

The Duchess stared at her.

"How so?"

"Your husband – the Duke – is dead."

The Duchess paled; for a moment, she stood speechless, and tears, real tears, flooded her blue eyes.

"*Dead?*"

"Murdered," said the Queen.

"Murdered? No. No, it cannot be. I must see him! Take me to where he is!" the Duchess cried.

The Black Queen came to her and took both her hands in hers.

"I would! If only…. But, no. It is too late; far too late, for that. And I fear – I'm so sorry to have to tell you – I fear that those whom you took to be your friends, those in whom you placed a trust most unmerited and unwise – were responsible. *Yes, my Duchess – I am so sorry. Your husband is dead. He fell at the hands of the Knave, and his Knight.*"

Chapter 15

POWER IS ALL

Ava.

The girl looked across the table, then turned away; Abby's hands rested lightly on the old wood, with her fingers touching the cards spread in a wide arc before her.

Light gilded tier after tier of books lining the walls of the Hythe house library. Soon it would be dusk; uneasily, the girl watched the sun set.

'Is this my last sunset?

Soon we will go; soon Cass and I must go 'Under'.'

Ava roused and turned to Abby.

"I'm sorry, Abby. What did you say?"

"I said – you must choose a card now."

Abby regarded the young woman whose hair was crimson in the late day's light. Cass would be here momentarily, Abby knew. For now, here was Ava, ready to choose a card.

'She is still distant; still lost in it.

Of course she is. That and so much more…'

"You seemed a million miles away," Abby said.

"I think I was, for a moment," the young woman replied.

"Where were you, Ava? Tell me – where are you now?"

Ava Fitzalan, the girl linked by blood to the child-thing at the grave, the girl who had somehow found a hole in time and space, became quite still. With her eyes focused on a place not in this room, with her thoughts on a memory not of this, nor of any other time – she spoke.

"At the Castle, in the dark; before the altar stone – He came. He came and He stood there, before me – I saw Him as plainly as I see you now. He is not tall, not much taller than I am. But, somehow splendid – regal, untouched by this age, by any age. He spoke to me – I can't tell you what He said now, it wasn't English – I know it wasn't. He spoke – and I knew. I knew what I had to do – whom I had to find. I would go back to the grave, and see **her** again. **'And he would come – the one who was necessary, the one who is to follow.'** That is what He said. It was only then – as I turned away

178

from Him, away from the altar stone, as I turned to leave, that I realised it. I had been standing there, under the trees, beside that stone – in utter darkness and that – from His robes to the silver diadem on His brow, to the skin on His face – I could see right through Him."

As if drawn there, eager to hear her words, the failing light hung over the two women at the table. Abby's eyes were bright; her voice low, still low – and commanding.

"Thank you, Ava, I see now– and you, you no longer need to, do you not?"

Sharply, the girl looked up, back at Abby and her gaze was once more clear, and untroubled.

"What have I been raving about? Here; I choose this one."

The girl's long fingers found the card, and she turned it face up; Abby studied it and laid out the rest of the Tree.

"You have chosen The Charioteer. See the One who commands the steeds, the steeds with their wings held aloft. The One who commands is a Woman; see how she holds the orb of enlightened *action in one hand – and in the other, the sword. See how she has gained a crown."*

"They are not horses, are they, Abby? The creatures that draw the Chariot; they seem familiar," Ava said.

"Indeed, they may be – to you! None now can say – perhaps these images were as close as they dared come – to the Gryphon, the one who shields what is priceless, the Lord and Protector against evil, against Magic of the blackest sort. Listen now, Ava, and remember this – ascendancy, Ava, ascendancy. The cards ascend through the deck – they rise: in awareness, in power – in risk.

As we must all."

"Ava. Fitz; can you hear me, Fitz? Do something. Can you just nod or spit – anything?"

The girl on the ground sighed deeply; the young man beside her did likewise, immeasurably relieved when she finally opened her eyes and saw him beside her, rubbing more salve onto her bare arm.

She shook her head, as if flinging off the last fleeting remnants of dream, and regarded first him, then the salve closely.

"How did you know it would work?" she asked and he smiled.

"How did you know the rope would hold?"

Propped up by a fire, with her sleeves rolled up to her shoulders, the Knight watched Cass gently apply another layer of the liniment to the skin of her arm.

Angry welts just moments ago, the bruises continued to lessen. Yet still, the marks from the Dark Queen's hand were apparent – like claw prints across the Knight's skin. The girl's arm ached acutely and she was still light-headed.

I was lucky – to have made it this far.

The Thane's men had followed their leader into the Wood; no one remained to hinder the Knight and the Knave and they had raced unhampered from the Duchess' house. Not entirely surprised to find that outside the building, calm day still held dominion, they had sped across the landscaped lawns, and passed into the forest. The Knight had set a furious pace, one so furious that

Cass had nearly collided with her when, without warning, she had stopped dead in her tracks.

She had turned to him. Ava's face was contorted in pain, her cheeks white, her pupils dilated. She pulled off her gloves with shaking hands, and stumbling, began to wander up the path, almost as one blind.

By the time he reached her, she was struggling to stand. Leaning against a tree and drenched with sweat, the girl was trying vainly to loosen her tunic. It was too much. Before his eyes, her legs gave way and he caught her up, into his arms, as she collapsed.

She had roused to the sound of his voice and the scent of fire.

Her sword stood point down in the turf a few steps away. Cass moved to feed the little blaze, then returned to her side. Circled by its sturdy stone moat, both the sight and the warmth of the fire were welcome to the stricken girl.

The Queen. The Black Queen.

It's not just Her eyes – Her touch can kill.

The salve, in its small sculpted box, lay near the fire; his wand lay beside it on the turf. With his own tunic removed, his sleeves rolled up, Cass now chafed her forehead and wrists with liquor from his flask, until her breathing strengthened and the girl's face brightened in hue. He sat back on his heels, watching her. Ava lay sprawled at full length before the fire with her cloak aside, and her soft shirt was open, her throat and chest exposed, whiter than the shirt, like ivory. They were in a small dell; around them tilted the toppled remnants of dead trees, some of them massive. The fallen giants stretched in twisted ruin, forming a natural enclave, both concealing – and defensible.

Cass carefully replaced the box's cover, then returned the thing to the bag that lay open at his feet. The Mage did not bother to look inside the sac itself; he was marveling less and less, not only at the salve's remarkable efficacy, but also in the nature of the sac that had held it.

It was still an unfathomable thing. He and the Knight had quickly learned that the elegantly tooled leather sacs they wore were mysterious in the extreme. Looking inside revealed nothing – the bags appeared empty. Only softly tooled leather, fragrant and smooth, met the eye. Yet, once closed, through

183

the leather itself – one could easily feel that there were objects within.

It was true each time: when the Knight had needed rope, when he had found the first card, and now – desperate for something, anything that would mitigate the ravages of the Black Queen's touch – the seeker had found what was needed in the pouch, even when both sacs were patently empty upon close examination at any other time.

It works only at need. The thing works only at need.

A low sound drew him back. He looked up. Unsteady but determinedly, Ava was pulling herself up, fumbling clumsily for her cloak.

He rose and immediately took it away from her.

"What do you think you're doing?" he asked.

"I'm feeling much better – we should go on."

"No."

"No?"

"*No,*" he said.

The light was beginning to give way. The soft rustle of leaf and branch was coupled now with new sounds, alarming ones – the sounds of living things.

He looked around the little dell that had suddenly become a camp. The trees ringed it closely; tall and dark, their heavy boughs formed a living wall against the threat of the deep Wood.

Night things are about.

But we have fire – and more.

He knelt, and placed the cloak about her; her regard was grave.

"You will stay here, I think," he said.

"Is that your 'command'?" she asked, finally.

For many moments, he said nothing.

"It is my *wish*," he replied slowly.

His tone was gentle.

But the Mage did not smile; she never took her eyes off him.

She was thinking; recalling how she had sat, all unknowing, beside something that had seemed to be the Duchess, that had seemed to be a *woman* – but was not. She was thinking of savage words in her mind, the terrible growling utterances, corrupt, seductive and hateful – commands that had called to her, called to lead her farther and farther away, along a dark path, at the end of which a figure, shadowed, horrific yet unknown – waited.

It was waiting – for me.
Knowing that he would follow.
Dark It was.
Hungry; eager – for fresh blood, for greater
power – new life.

She was thinking of the moment that other words had come into her mind, words that forced themselves into her like hot fingers, like fire – words that had opened a floodgate of sensations, of need – of desire. In her mind now was the memory of that desire, to hear – to obey. With that knowledge had come a release, a shock, as of sensual pleasure, deep and penetrating; a thralldom as captivating, as arousing, as it had been commanding.

It was the Mage that had called her; the Sorcerer that had spoken; her one wish had been to grant all of his. In the house, her appearance of being lost, ravished, and overcome was not appearance only – it had been the manifestation of fact.

His will grows strong.
What could he not command one to do?
What could he not command me to do?

I wanted to please him – to answer his every whim.

I wanted to obey him – I wanted ….

Now she regarded him; so close, so mystifying, so compelling. Here was the man whose words alone had called her back from the Queen's dark chant, the man who watched her now – the man whose eyes burned as he looked at her, who still did not smile as she spoke, haltingly, weakly, as if recalling a dark, terrible dream.

"That moment, when I looked straight into Her eyes – what I saw was darkness. You, the room, everything went away. There was nothing; just me – I was alone in the dark – with *Her. With It, for that form She has taken is but one of Its shapes, and is nothing close to true.* It was whispering my name. Suddenly, I heard you speak; I could see again. *Then, all I could see – was you."*

He had remained frozen where he was, on his knees, silently watching her.

"Are you afraid of me?"

He had appraised her very thoughts, the unspoken fear. She looked away.

Without warning, the Mage moved – he drew near, stretching himself down, lying beside her and his face was very close to hers.

His shirt was open almost to the waist. Firelight played across the muscles of his chest and the smooth, bare skin of his arms. The man's features bore evidence of the time passed here – *Under* – and all that had occurred. The light beard on his face was startling – not merely older and not just in appearance, something had changed within him. A great weariness overcame her.

"Are you afraid of me?" he asked again.

"No," she breathed. "I will never be afraid of you."

A light shone from his eyes. His hand drew near her cheek, his fingers gently tracing across her lips; the Knight's eyelids fluttered and her voice was low, almost incoherent.

"It lives – but It does not rule here. It lives – solely because of the *other*. The *other*...."

"Ava – Ava, what 'other'?" he exclaimed softly; it was too late, the Knight's eyes were closed.

The Mage rose to his feet. Now he stood over the girl, straddling her form between his legs and he looked down upon her, his eyes stern, his jaw set. The sleeping one turned, and her hand reached across her side – where it drew near the Mage's wand on the turf – the wand from whose tip a soft, blue brilliance had once more begun to curl.

Cass' eyes went from one to the other – from the sleeping Knight, to the wand with its pale warning. Then he stepped over the girl, and retrieved his weapon, its light fading as it came back to his hand. He crossed to the far side of the fire. There, the Sorcerer drew his dagger, and, wrapped in his own cloak, he settled himself against a thick trunk.

There he remained, watchful, lost in thought, limned against the light of the small blaze. The day passed and full dark pressed close. Night descended in the dell – the Mage's wand lay across his lap.

Ŧ

The sensation of something firm at the back of her neck roused the Knight from deep slumber.

Damn tree roots.

Ribbons of pale light found their way through the trees and into the dell. The fire was little more than red coals.

Ava shifted; what she had taken for a tree root was Cass' arm. She lay cradled against him, his body curled behind hers.

He was not asleep. His lips moved against the hair that tumbled over her ear.

"Don't move. We've got company."

"I thought I'd heard them all."

"No. I mean it," he said. "There's someone at the edge of the glade."

"Well, we can't just stay here, like this, all day!"

His laughed softly.

"Speak for yourself! But, on my mark…"

At his word, she rolled from him, freed her sword and leapt to her feet. The Mage was no longer on the ground where they had lain – Cass was up, his own sword drawn, as a volley of black arrows pierced the spot they had left, pinning Ava's cloak to the ground.

The Mage's flask was out – he hurled its contents onto the fire's coals and flames shot skyward. The two leapt behind the blaze as three men, garbed and masked in ebony, with swords drawn – darted at them from the cover of the trees.

Just as the nearest one reached him, Cass dropped to the ground; his outstretched legs tumbled his man onto the turf. Ava saw the flash of his blade as the Knave drove his sword deep into the man's chest. He turned as the third attacker flew at him, sending them both to the ground. There they struggled, rising to fight hand to hand, until the Mage wounded his man. Cass' sword hilt dropped his attacker like a stone.

The Knight's own blade moved in a shining arc of light as she feinted a blow, then parried her own attacker's lunge. The glade rang with the sound of blade on blade until a misstep took the girl stumbling backward. In a flash, her attacker was upon her. Flat on her back, she fought now with both sword and dagger – the two combatants rose, and fell, and rolled, fighting savagely. The Knight's blades glittered like shards of light, until a fierce kick from her boot sent the man flying backward.

He landed squarely on the fire. He pulled himself free, but his tunic was scorched and smoking as the Knight reached him and sent her sword into him. Ava stood over him – from the corner of her eye, she saw the last attacker rising up, directly behind Cass. The Knight cried out and the Mage dropped just as her thrown dagger passed over his head.

Yet, even wounded, the Black Queen's assassin, the last one standing, was quick and determined. He flung off the Knight's thrown knife with his gauntlet.

Pulling his own dagger, the man threw it with all his force – directly at Ava's face.

Cass had rolled aside; now he leapt up.

In a flash, the Mage's arm rose.

His hand extended, his fingers spread wide – and the very air came alive, not just that encircling the Mage's hand, but also the air directly before the face of the Knight.

Like a hanging pool of utterly transparent fluid, the air before the girl writhed and rippled – and the dagger froze in its path, inches from Ava's face, seemingly imbedded in a thick but barely visible wall made up of the air itself.

The attacker muttered a harsh curse; his astonishment was nothing compared with that of the Mage and the Knight.

Cass' breath came out in a rush – the dagger dropped to the ground. The man who had thrown it took to his heels. In panic-driven flight, he disappeared down an overgrown and shadowy path, leading away from the dell.

For the space of two heartbeats, Cass stared at his hand, then at the Knight.

"Come on!" he shouted. "We've got to stop him!"

The two swept up their gear and tore down the path after him.

Chapter 16

TUNNEL/VISION

Speed was imperative. Speed was impossible.

For barely discernible and densely overgrown, the path gave the two as much use of their weapons now as when they had been in the thick of the ambush in the dell. Cass cursed under his breath.

It allows him passage – just as it impedes us now. Does Her will reach this far?

Trailing off, its last echoes coming from the distance ahead, the sound of a man's scream brought them to a standstill.

What followed after, other than the noise of their laboured breathing – was dead silence. Like a tide, it flowed around them, eerie, all encompassing, palpable.

Like the silence in my room – when Her card began to change.

Like the silence in the pine glade and in the Duchess' house.

When silence falls here – all Hell is about to break loose.

The trees about them grew more and more sparse, replaced by a profusion of shrubs and vines. They pushed their way forward. In moments, they had left the forest behind and came to a halt.

With stout vines trailing over its top and sides, and laden with moss and ferns, a rough wall was before them.

It was extremely wide and high, with curving sides made of pieced, heavy grey stones. Built directly into it, a high, arching doorway soared, with a thick wooden door that hung ajar.

Beyond the door, a dark stone tunnel could be glimpsed; a second door was barely seen, also ajar, at the tunnel's far side. A fine layer of loose stone and sand stretched in a narrow line along the ground beside the outside of the wall itself.

In the lead, the Knight started forward. But her companion put out his arm to bar her way.

"Listen."

"God," she said. "There's nothing."

"Again."

Rich and varied, the sounds of living, if not wholesome forest, could still be heard, but faintly now. These real sounds came from behind them, from the trees at their backs. A bright sky was overhead, and a faint distant sound of falling water could be heard. But here, about this place – was nothing.

The Knight readied her sword and the Knave his own blade. They drew close to the arching doorway with its tunnel, straining to see beyond it, past the shadows, into the land beyond.

"On the other side – it's a garden," he whispered.

"*Her* garden."

Still was deep, brooding silence, like that of a held breath, or the terrible stillness of the unquiet, tenanted tomb, and the Knight regarded the high, wide wall.

"Did he pass through here?"

"If he did, then we must as well."

"I don't usually see demons in dust bunnies – but I *really* don't like this, Cass," Ava muttered suddenly.

He, too, studied the wall and the tunnel. The door was wide and solid – it moved easily on its hinges. Inside the tunnel, thin shafts of light penetrated the solid pieced stones that lined the walls and curving ceiling. The Knave frowned; along the tunnel's floor, unevenly spaced small piles of dry, grey dust lay strewn, as if someone had emptied their dustpans in little heaps. Scattered along the floor, dim in this light, he could also make out what seemed to be old moss fragments or bits of dry, old vines, close to the piles of dust. With their wood nearly rotted through and in rusted, iron housings, dry oil brands were spaced along the tunnel's cold walls, protruding like dark, skeletal ribs.

"Can't imagine why; it's dark, and creepy. Other than that, it looks like a fun place."

"For about two seconds. Is there any other way over this wall?"

"It's a steep slope, but I think we should try it."

He set down his gear. Then he approached the wall and, taking hold of one of the many stout vines that coursed over its side, pulled himself up onto its curving stones.

The Knave made good progress. He had nearly reached the top when the vine in his hands began to move, twisting violently. He struggled to keep hold of it when, with a deliberate, savage movement, the vine pulled itself free, sending him tumbling down to the ground. From there, Cass gaped up at the wall – as it began to shudder and quake until the entire length was moving and grating before them.

A thin rain of dust and small stones pattered down. The wall grew still and Cass looked up at it.

"Let me rephrase that – I don't think we should try it."

Ava now came to the wall; her hand reached out. Before her fingers could touch even the moss on its surface, the wall shuddered again.

"Bad wall! *Damn.* The only way through, is in."

She returned to the door – it was now swinging on its hinges – swinging back and forth, even though the wall no longer moved. The girl froze, peering inside.

"Cass – get over here."

He came to her – and he heard them, too –

harsh words were rising from the dark wood of the door itself.

> *It opens – See! The path is wide,*
> *Perhaps you'll reach the other side.*
> *It closes – Woe! The path grows long,*
> *If answer given should be wrong!*
> *Not Key nor Card shall passage win,*
> *Seek Light from where it hides – within.*
> *In might, in strength, how he shall fail;*
> *In fear, in doubt, shall she prevail?*
> *Thy blood and bone feed wood and stone.*
> *A second's pause, a moment's wait,*
> *Shall bring swift death – or open gate.*

Cass closely perused the door, then the tunnel.

"Cheery. Wait – now, will you look at that?" he breathed.

Beyond, at the far end of the tunnel, the door leading out still stood ajar. Ava looked again, and a chill came over her.

The length of the tunnel is not constant.

From moment to moment – it grows longer and shorter.

Something about that floor – the dirt piled along the way….

"Cass. Will you take up the wand?"

He gave her a sharp look; however, when he drew it forth, it lay still and quiet across his palm.

"I feel nothing," he said, and returned the weapon to its place in his belt.

The Knight took a deep breath, then her gloved hand determinedly met the door and she pressed upon it – with a soft creak, the door swung on its rusting hinges, swung wide – and admitted them.

They stepped across the threshold; now they stood completely inside the tunnel. The Knight whispered.

"Wait. We should prop the door open somehow…"

Her words came too late. In a flash, the door had swung firmly shut behind them. Any chance of exiting through the door had now utterly vanished.

So had every evidence of light.

Amazement filled the Mage – he could see his hands and body, as though he stood in dim moonlight. Yet, around him reigned utter darkness – and there was no sign of the Knight.

"Cass!" she cried, her voice echoing as from a distance. "Where are you?" That voice held a note of panic; it was a panic not unshared by her companion. "I can see myself – but not you. Cass?"

"I'm right here – right beside you. You can't see me, either, can you?" he exclaimed. He reached out; under his hands, he suddenly felt the arm of the girl. Blindly, but with both hands, he found her shoulders, still astonished that despite her nearness, she was yet invisible to the eye. His outstretched arms seemed to end on nothing, hanging before him in mid-air. Then, he felt her hands on him, on his chest, about his shoulders – but to his eyes, nothing stood beside him.

"Astonishing," Ava whispered. "Can you feel the walls? Can you see the door at the other end?"

"No. Fitz, I'm going to let go of you for a second, don't move."

"As if," she grumbled.

He reached again for his wand; it came easily from his belt. Then, to his horror – the weapon seemed to move, shuddering in his grip. It then slipped through his fingers, falling soundlessly to the ground, to land somewhere at his feet, on ground as invisible as the walls around them.

He cursed.

"Okay. What?" demanded the Knight.

"I dropped it! Or, rather the thing practically jumped from my hand. I can't see it – I can't see it to find it. It's somewhere on the ground."

"Bloody Hell."

The Mage reached for his bag, then stopped – the words they had heard at the tunnel's door came back to him.

Nor Key nor Card shall passage win …

"We need light – light, Ava, have you anything that will give us light?"

Under her bare hands, her own sac felt empty. It came to her like lightning, her hand seemed drawn – to land full upon the hilt of the ivory baton. Carefully, she drew the thing from her belt. Her fingers roved over its surface and in her mind, she saw it as clear as if it lay brightly lit upon her palm.

Strange. I wonder now – so much has happened, and so quickly – but how is it that I never thought to look at this thing, I never thought of drawing this – as a weapon? I do so now.

But how can I do this? What must I do?

I am no sorcerer; I have no power.

How can I use such a thing – I am but a warrior.

The ivory felt warm, its runes of silver bright and glowing in her mind's eye. The wand lay in her hand. Now sensation crept across her skin, engulfing her arm. She raised the slim wand, full of admiration for the delicate carving, its wondrous marriage of bone and metal.

The Knight drew a deep breath, for, without warning, a flood of words had come into her head, words only half-understood – only half-heard, as indistinct as the images that gripped her suddenly.

She stood upon a great moor, feeling the embrace of the wind's fingers about her waist.

Cold air streamed past her face, lifting her hair, ruffling the tops of the gorse and heather that

grew in profusion, stretching away, far out of sight.
Against the stormy, light- washed sky, their leaves
and stems were a kaleidoscope of colour – amber,
blue, russet and gold.

In the distance, from out of the low clouds –
the bird appeared.

Slowly, as if it hung upon the air, the hawk
glided lower, toward her and she gazed on its
majestic wings, spread wide as it coursed nearer. On
the hill beyond, in air that seemed fractured and
indistinct, the hawk drew up. As it did so, its form
began to change – light engulfed the great raptor and
out of that light, as it came to the ground – the Man
appeared – and she heard His voice.

'The Season of Fire, the Fire that seeks and
awakens the sleeping world.

The Year turns.

The Sun rises to bring again life to the land,
with light, with fire.

Awaken with it.

Lēoht.'

Now He was coming up the hill toward her,
the wind lifting His rough cloak, lifting it to reveal

the coloured robes beneath – the robes of the
Wizard.

"My Master – I wait," she replied as He came
up, standing before her and she saw that the light in
His eyes was as bright as the jewels that were woven
into the silver circlet He wore on His brow.

"Lēoht," she said aloud, still not
comprehending, as warmth surged through her like
a flaming tide, as rich, as exhilarating as the tide that
passion itself unleashes.

"Ava!" came Cass' shout, close by – but all
dimmed beside the overwhelming sensations that
coursed through her, before the brilliance erupting
from the wand, until the young woman herself stood
bathed in a circle of radiance.

Panting, gasping for breath, instantaneously,
she could see – Cass was beside her with his wand in
his hand, and with his shout, the dead, dry fibers of
every brand along the walls of their dark prison
burst into incandescent flames.

They stood side by side in wonder. With eyes
wide and parted lips and a radiant sheen of moisture
on her throat and face, the young woman looked at
the Mage.

"What happened?" the Mage asked.

"What did you see?" she replied, when she had recovered the power of clear speech.

"I was calling your name – I heard you speak; I couldn't understand a word of it. Suddenly there you were. Suddenly there was light."

The girl stared at the thing in her hand, still warm to the touch, and so it remained until the moment she returned it to her belt.

He looked at her. She was still distant from him, somehow otherworldly, still apart from where they now stood. Her cheeks were flushed; her pupils seemed enormous, unnaturally black and wide in the light of the brands whose flames crackled brightly along the walls.

And seeing her – the Mage was aroused – by the sight of her there, still spellbound, with her face and hair lit by an aura only he could see.

The Knight's face paled suddenly; head bowing, she slowly slid down until she was on her knees on the tunnel floor. Once again, the Mage stood over her, engulfed by emotions and sensations that threatened so nearly to escape his will. He knelt close beside her. Desire rose in him again and he was nearly overcome by need – to touch her, to feel her under his hands.

Under my hands – under my control.

As I felt at the house of the Duchess

when I invoked the Word.

Enchantment – the Knight has felt it.

She has seen.

Now – she knows.

The young woman's head raised and she looked at him, wordlessly. He said nothing; he helped her rise to her feet.

"Let's get out of here," she said, and they started forward again.

Chapter 17

TIME OF THEIR LIVES

Yet, forward was not progress – the door at the far end of the tunnel was now clearly shut.

Worse now, the tunnel seemed endless. The air was cold, the walls were cold; cold trickled like melting ice from the slick grey surfaces of the walls, walls that seemed to close in upon them. With a rising sense of alarm, they began to run. Yet, even after running what should have been a substantial way, they seemed to have covered less than half the distance to reach the door.

They halted, breathless.

"It takes all the running you can do – to stay in the same place," gasped the Knight bitterly, to Cass' look. "That is what the Red Queen told Alice."

"And to actually get somewhere?"

"You must run twice as fast."

"Great."

Undaunted, they had just started forward again, when beside them, from the wall itself – there came a dull, grinding sound.

One of the large stones close by their heads had begun to quiver. Little by little, it loosened from its place; then, utterly defiant of any law of gravity – it slowly floated out into the space of the tunnel.

There the stone hung in the air; wisps of frigid, grey mist crept about it.

From the hole that remained, a small shred of something pale appeared; it moved out of the hole with a low, rustling sound – and floated down, landing on the tunnel floor. They saw then that what had appeared from the tunnel's mouth to be piles of dried moss, were in fact shreds of cloth – molding, rotting, and falling to pieces as they found sudden freedom from the grip of cold, damp stone.

The space that had lain behind the stone was utterly dark, penetrating far into the wall.

It was not empty.

From deep within the hole, came a grating – a soft scraping, as of something moving or pushing forward. The Knave gasped – coming into view, creeping slowly to the edge of the hole, were the long, dry fingers of a hand – nothing but bone and grey sinew remained to show that it might once have been almost human. Sere and green with age, more cloth shreds appeared at the hole's mouth, pushed forward by fingers long dead, animated into hellish life. These bits reached the lip of the hole, fluttering to the ground at their feet, dissolving into fine, grey, ashy dust, adding to the heaps that ranged along the floor.

Ava cried out – for from some great distance within the shadows of the hole,came now terrible echoes – the sounds of gnawing – the slow, terrible grating of teeth as they scraped on bone. At her cry– the gnawing ceased – something was dragging itself forward, moving closer and closer to the aperture that opened into the tunnel.

Up and down the length of the tunnel, one by one – other blocks had began to move, pulling free from their housings. More and more apertures opened. In terror, the Knight and the Knave ran, in desperation to reach the door at the tunnel's far end. But the tunnel was still utterly endless, and uncountable now the stones loosening one by one from the wall, each ready to disgorge its testimony of undying hunger and fearsome living decay.

The brands on the walls sputtered with the speed of their flight, and such was their speed that they were powerless to stop themselves from slamming headlong into the tunnel's far door, appearing from nowhere. Yet somehow, there it was right before them; they had reached the end. Shaken and bruised, they hauled themselves up to stand before a door that was shut, utterly immovable even to their combined efforts to force it open. The Knight glanced behind them, down the length of the tunnel. She cried out again. Now she redoubled her frantic strikes on the door and Cass heard her desperate words as they alternated with the furious blows of her sword, which drew sparks from the metal studs in the door that she struck.

"Leave here, leave now – or it will be too late – we will never leave at all."

The door held.

He too, looked behind. From far down the long passageway, darkness was now creeping – like a foul growth, tendrils reached along the floor, along the walls, and as they neared – each brand flickered, sputtered and went out. Out of that darkness, which soon engulfed the walls and curving top of the tunnel – pale eyes peered out, and now there were hundreds of them. The livid stones hung in frigid space, a space that reeked of the open tomb, and unholy light streamed from the apertures.

"My Knight – hold!"

The girl froze – and now, in the silence, they heard it – a low chant was again coming from the wood itself.

> *'A second's pause, a moment's wait,*
> *Choose now: swift death or open gate.*
> *Thy blood and bone feed wood and stone.*
> *What wouldst Thou?'*

"What do we say?" she asked in desperation

He faced the door squarely. "We wish to leave."

The door remained closed.

> *'Thy blood and bone feed wood and stone.*
> *What wouldst Thou?'* came its somber

request.

The Mage tried again. "We wish to enter the garden."

> *'What wouldst Thou?'*

The darkness was nearing them, soon it would be at their heels; still, the door remained unresponsive to either word or weapon. Both now quaked with the cold; the stench of the tunnel was overwhelming, there was no air left to breathe.

The Knight stepped forward.

"We wish to enter *Her* garden."

Still nothing; distraught, the Knight renewed her attack on the door, smashing vainly at the wood with her sword's hilt.

Thy blood and bone.

As her sword's edge flew past him, his hand shot out – and the Mage took hold of the naked blade with his bare hand. His grip stopped it in its savage arc – and blood ran down the blade, blood ran down the hand and arm of the Mage. The Sorcerer turned to the door.

"We Will Enter Her Garden."

Reaching out, he placed his bleeding palm directly against the wood – there, down and across the door's grainy surface – his blood trickled down.

The door gave a mighty shudder; with the sound of wood creaking and splintering, it opened outward, allowing just enough room for the two prisoners to squeeze through.

They fell forward outside onto the ground, choking, forcing air into their lungs – and through the half- open door on the cavern floor, darkness was now pooling, reaching, still insatiate, still seeking.

The Mage hauled himself up onto his knees. He reached up and slammed his bloody hand against the door – and creaking and moaning, it closed against the shadows massing within.

Cass fell backward onto the ground. On the wood of the door, his bloody handprint was already fading, the fresh blood vanishing into the wood, as rain vanishes into parched and thirsty sand. Barely able to breathe, shaken and wondering as to whether they could even return by this path – the two lay for a moment on the ground. Then they rose to their feet and stumbled forward, away from the monstrous wall.

They stood upon a groomed path of mossy, cobbled stones. Before them was indeed a garden, richly planted. Wild it seemed in places, in others with carefully tended, raised beds. It was a garden vast and seemingly borderless in its extent.

This is the place – Her place.

What the Gryphon showed me, a place without borders.

Endless with possibilities.

Why did I not see that before – the endless possibilities?

Here are Her flowers, with their scents all wrong.

Now I see, I understand – they are just different.

There, in the distance, were orchids – as beautiful as Abby's favourites – here, the blooms twisted, and their contorted petals opened a foot across. A light breeze stirred bromeliads into motion, setting aquiver the long blue flowers that cascaded down from their red bracts and their sepals parted in the breeze.

Like wolves' jaws, they hung down twice as long as a man's hand.

Like wolves' jaws, the sepals were ringed with teeth.

"Cass – don't move."

He had learned not to question. The Knight's sword was drawn. He froze.

Coming closer now, moving with uncanny precision, it lowered. Coming into view, it halted just beside his cheek.

It was the face of a dragon.

Chapter 18

AS DREAMS ARE MADE OF

It was the face of a dragon – apparently suspended in mid-air. In confusion, the Mage stared at it.

Not a dragon – a flower.
But alive.

The petals of a huge flower formed its face. There were eyes in that face – moving, large and golden-green – and the Snap Dragon scrutinised Cass closely, avidly.

The warm breath of the thing was on his skin. A flash of live flame flickered at the Snap Dragon's whiskered mouth, a mouth that showed no inclination to ignite with the heat. The mouth opened wider – it, too, was a mouth lined with long, sharp teeth.

The Mage stayed motionless; the skin on his face grew warm.

It was not from the breath of the monstrous creature, with flaming mouth, with its bare teeth, that hovered, poised beside him. His face burned from what had now formed in the air before his forehead – the image of the quincunx.

The Mage did not see this thing as it moved, slowly rotating, pulsing with light, with its many glowing sides, all joining together as one in the centre.

The Dragon, however, saw all.

The Snap Dragon studied the young man's face carefully. Its head turned to the Knight.

Now the long neck came into view; scaled and green, like living bark. At the top of its more than ten- foot length, claw-like leaves hung down, like branches, but deadly, for at the end of the arm stalks, their talons opened and closed, curling in the breeze.

Its voice resounded, at once silky and sonorous.

"I did not believe. Yet, it is true. He said you would come."

"He?" Ava asked.

"Gryphon."

The girl frowned.

"Did my Lord petition?"

The creature drew nearer.

"A pledge has been offered – for now," it said.

"And a covenant?" asked the Knight.

A strange, keening sigh came from the Great One's dark lips.

"Agreed – for now," it replied. The Dragon's face rose up, higher, until it once more hovered over Cass' head.

But suddenly two more heads, smaller than the first drew near. More and more appeared and they circled and entwined about one another. Fire filled the air – hot and deadly, palpable to those on the ground, and a flurry of sibilant sounds, harsh with anger, with fear and hatred, erupted in the torrid thicket.

A volley of hisses and harsh words – the Knight and the Knave could do nothing, powerless to move or intercede in a debate which clearly meant either life or death – theirs.

"They must die! *They must live!*" came the angry speeches. "*The pledge was made!* Covenant was agreed! But not by all!"

Brazen and terrifying rose the discord over the heads of the humans; the air seethed with snarling, and with deafening peals of sound. The flaming jaws of one of the monsters suddenly lowered, its maw gaping and brilliant with flame.

"Die! They die now!" the thing growled.

The head reared back – then the Dragon launched its fearsome jaws straight at the Mage.

"Nay!" cried their defender. "They must live!"

From the defending Dragon's jaws came a bubbling, flaming spear of liquid – spewing directly into the face of the attacker. A piercing cry rose into the air as first, the victim's face, then, the rough, scaly length of neck burst into flames. Crackling tongues of fire coursed down the stalk, a scent like that of burning incense filled the air.

In seconds, all that remained of the attacker was a blackened stump of neck, crumbling into hot, smoking ash floating in the air, drifting down onto the ground, and its roots, charred and pulled from the ground, curling into dark twisted stubs. The mouths of the remaining Dragons closed. They lowered their fearsome heads and a soft, submissive crooning filled the air.

In answer, a brazen blast came from their defender's throat. Then it curled its neck, and the blooming creature brought its face to rest, inches away from Cass' face.

"Dost Thou know, Mage, what drives this bloodshed? Whence comes this hate and fear?"

"No, my Lord," breathed the Mage; the Dragon bowed its head and spoke.

> *'A Flame that stands – a bitter knife;*
> *Shall mercy spare the Mage's life?*
> *In chambers dark, secure both Light,*
> *And Fire – seek the Elemental's might.*
> *Comes now the time when fall She must.*
> *Shall **all** then fall down – into dust?*
> *We fear – what little shall remain?*
> *Through you comes freedom – loss and pain.'*

The Dragon's head rose up again; the other beasts keened sadly. Cass breathed deeply.

"May my Lord – accept my humble thanks." Then the Mage stepped away from the grove of flames, seeing only then that the Knight was lowering her sword – it had remained at the height of Cass' face, held there, poised and ready, throughout the confrontation.

"What else is here – that has teeth?" she wondered. Before he could say 'What doesn't?' he felt her grip on his arm.

Further, down the cobbled path, the grounds opened up into a wider, stone lined space.

There, protruding from below the dense vegetation just beside the path – motionless on the ground – were the soles and heels of two black boots.

Ŧ

He was not yet quite dead when they reached him.

Prone, on his back on the ground, the last of the Queen's assassins lay. With face pale, and his eyes closed, his eyelids fluttered restlessly as though he was in deep dream, and his breath came in increasingly shallow pants.

His features were contorted in agony.

He did not awaken; he did not attempt to rise, nor could he – his body was wrapped head to foot in green, laced with taut, emerald-hued vines.

Fragile and lovely were the vine's flowers adorning his body like wreaths; pure, white and almost iridescent. From where they stood, both Knave and Knight could smell the fragrance that hung over him like a cloud – heavy, sweet, intoxicating.

"Nightshade," Ava whispered. "It's Nightshade."

"Where in Hell have you ever seen Nightshade like that?"

"Here; only here – in Hell."

Do not sleep.

Cass shook his head; the Knave's eyes flashed open suddenly – he exhaled violently, overcome with the sense of imminent danger.

What is happening?

Do not sleep!

Beside him, Ava was silent, her breathing slowed. She sighed, her head drooping. Her eyelids finally closed. Suddenly, Cass was shaking her violently. She tottered forward; he dragged her up, pulling her away from the man mercilessly wrapped at their feet.

"Fitz! Wake up – Don't breathe it, don't breathe, don't breathe the fragrance! Fitz!"

She coughed. As though rousing from sleep, she shook off her languor – the sweet scent had brought lethargy, numbing, and calming. The Mage shook her again then he struck her hard across the face, forcing her to breathe, pulling her yet further away. She struggled against him, feeling still the need to sit, to rest, to sleep – feeling still the hypnotising effects of the deadly perfume that had nearly overpowered them, as it had clearly overpowered the man dying on the ground.

For he was dying – as if held fast by dream, the one sent by the Black Queen to kill them wrestled vainly and helplessly in sleep, his breath coming more and more slowly.

Yet while he still breathed, while the spirit and power of his life yet remained strong within him – a dreadful metamorphosis was taking place.

Before their eyes, his face and hands grew steadily greyer, more livid.

Hollows appeared below his cheeks and the skin around his eyes waxed ghastly blue. With jaws slack then stiffening, his skin withered, shrinking in their sight. His mouth fell open, revealing gums pale, pulled back from his teeth. His skin blanched now, even as those vines that were most tightly wrapped, and closest to his heart seemed to swell, waxing richer and more vibrant in colour.

The Nightshade's perfume continued to fill the air, reaching a sickly sweet crescendo even as the breath of the man on the ground caught, and ceased utterly. Now dry, dusty and splintering was the flesh of the man on the ground; his clothing slowly sank over the crumbling bits of his body.

The Knight was still weak; Cass set her on her feet, then all at once, he lifted her bodily, carrying her further away, away from the corpse.

For, the leafy bonds, finished but not sated had begun to unravel.

Almost with the man's last breath, the waxy flowers quivered anew. Opening and closing as if the plant itself breathed, suddenly, the vine's tendrils, like long, dark magenta fingertips began to creep over the turf where the dead man lay – seeking, seeking the warmth of living flesh, the spark of still vital spirit.

When those tendrils quickly rose up like so many snake heads, eagerly testing the very air in their direction, Ava and Cass threw up their cloaks and leapt back.

It was barely in time – the plant itself moved, tendrils shot forward directly at them. They fastened on the Knight's cloak, nearly ripping it from her grasp, winding about it like green claws. Ava yanked the garment free and the two raced away from what remained on the ground, and the horror, poised and ravenous above it.

They flew along the path; turning, they found themselves entering a wide meadow ringed by giant trees overhead, whose thick canopy shaded the ground below. Cass caught his boot on something that protruded upward from the silky grass.

He toppled; stunned with the impact of his fall, he sprawled headlong on the ground. Dazed, he looked up; the Knight pulled him to his feet.

What had tripped him was a mushroom.

Chapter 19

SOUL AND SORROW

It was an enormous toadstool.

The hard, thick cap was low, but nearly yard wide. It was just the first of many. Before them, becoming a forest beneath the trees, spread a veritable jungle of fungi, many of the toadstools rising taller than a house, with monstrous round caps. A chaotic sea of colours met their eyes – rich rust, blue, pale pink. The mushrooms were rainbow hued, with fantastically curving and twisting trunks, and their enormous parasols cast deep shadows below their velvet dark ribs.

They were not alone in the forest of giants.

Just paces away, perched atop an enormous cap many yards wide and higher than their heads – a dark, rustling shape rose, stirring into appalling life. At the sound of their approach, the lumbering shape rose higher and higher, finally towering more than man high over the smooth, flat surface of the titan toadstool.

The Knave stared at the creature on the mushroom.

"I know," murmured the Knight. "And Gryphons do not exist. But what a Hell of a butterfly he'll make."

Her voice drew the thing's attention and it turned to face them. The creature's sheer size, along with the peculiarly intense look in its eyes made them shudder. Those eyes were round, saucer-like, and their dark, liquid surfaces were singularly inscrutable, like witching orbs. The smooth hide shone. Green, gold and palest blue; all played over the surface of its soft skin, and when the creature moved, so changed the colours of its skin, seeming now lighter, now darker to the eye.

"Who are you?" came its voice, low, yet clear, deep, like the murmur of coming storm.

"Who are you?" the Caterpillar asked again.

It curled its head downward. Then it moved toward them, alarmingly faster than its size might suggest. They caught sight of its hands, for hands they were, running up and down in rows, lining the Caterpillar's vast sides. They ended in simple claws, dark yet delicate as human fingers; the creature spoke again.

"What's the matter – Cat got your tongue? It's too soon in the story for that."

A dreadful low, chuckling gurgle came from the Caterpillar's proboscis, which extended out from its face a foot or more. Two long, black, serrated mandibles enclosed the proboscis. Soft, flexible feelers about its mouth quivered with humour, and the rigid mandibles, with their sharp red tips, made a clacking sound.

Its guests were not amused – they were immediately less so when a considerably smaller version of their inquisitor appeared at the rim of the toadstool. The diminutive larva crept along the lip of the cap, until it finally pulled itself atop the crown.

The Caterpillar saw it.

Its eyes grew even larger and now luminous.

In a flash, it lunged forward. Grasping its rival tightly with its clawed hands, the Caterpillar shook it savagely from side to side. Then, it sank its mandibles deep into the victim's soft flesh. The prey cried out with a low, wailing sob. Dark fluid trickled from the captive, oozing thickly over the cap and for several unbearable moments, a soft, lapping came from the giant killer's mouth.

It was all over in seconds. The shriveled carcass was summarily pushed over edge of the cap. The Caterpillar turned its attention once more to the Knight and the Knave, standing aghast below.

"Why do you frown?" it asked. "It wasn't a relative; at least – I don't think so. You should try one yourself – you might like it."

Its head once more dropped low. Busily, hands and feelers moved swiftly and rhythmically, as the great creature groomed itself. Its liquid gaze returned to them, and it spoke again.

"Now – who are you?"

The Knight took a deep breath; she approached the cap and the monstrosity astride it.

"I am called …"

"No, no. That's not how it's done, not at all. You should not tell me, not yet. That is sound advice anywhere, until you know to whom you are speaking. What are you doing here?"

The Mage joined the Knight.

"It would be unwise to tell."

232

The Caterpillar studied him with greater interest.

"Ah! It would, indeed; were it not for the fact that I already know full well your purpose, at least thus far. Yet, purposes are notorious things, you know. Before you look twice – they have changed. Yours will, too. But it's just *there*, you know."

"What is?"

The Caterpillar's feelers curled again and dark liquid roiled inside the creature's maw.

"Her palace; it's just beyond the Field, beyond the Falls. You pass by the Hatter's table, his fine little house, and then, why, you are practically at Her doorstep. You will find it all there, all of it – the Grand Salon, the Ebony Hall, and the Barracks. Yet, let us not forget the Dungeon; I think *that* may be the jewel. I have heard the Dungeon is rather *nice*. But *you* can tell me all about it, my good Mage."

"What makes you think I'll end there?"

"Because you must; where else will you end? And endings are simply another sort of beginning aren't they?"

"You're just a character in a book, you know," Ava said.

"*'Just'* – that's a tricky word – see how many things it means – and how many of them apply here. Perhaps I wrote the book, fair Knight. Besides, are you the same as the book that you hold in your hand?"

"No – of course not," she replied.

"Neither am I," the giant creature said.

"But, in the upper world…"

"Upper world, under world – one world, wouldn't you agree? *As above – so below.* You see? Reality – now, that's hard, isn't it?"

The Mage stepped closer.

"Wait – that's what she said – how do you know that?"

The Caterpillar chuckled again. Its liquid chortle faded away with the start of a high keening sound – with that sound, the entire surface of the mushroom's cap began to move.

The wide, velvety gills lining the underside of the parasol had begun to vibrate. A sibilant fluttering sound filled the air, like to that of the pages of a large book being ruffled. Before their eyes, the gills parted, and the air below the mushroom suddenly clouded with colour. Spores; softly glowing, prismatic, of pale opal and peach streamed from the mushroom's gills, and soon they enveloped both the cap and its tenant.

A light yet pervasive odor, musky and sweet filled the air; the visitors drew back, away from the pulsing cloud of scent and spectral light.

But, engulfed by it, the Caterpillar rose up. It stretched upright to its full monstrous length. It then curled its body, bathing in the clouds of colour with obvious delight, breathing audibly until the breeze carried away the spores. The mushroom's gills flattened again and closed; the creature turned once more to the Knight and the Knave.

"That is *so* much better," the thing exclaimed softly. "Now I can see clearly."

"Do you still see us?" the Knight asked.

"Why, of course! You, and he, as well."

"What else do you see?" the Knave prompted.

The Caterpillar stared off into the space above their heads and spoke dreamily.

"Oh, many things, marvelous things! The Servant – and the last Key; that one turns, you know. A great house in flames – but flames are not enough – *Her* heart is too strong, too cold. So it goes

– if you speak of the Devil, he comes to your door –
you *will* try to remember that, won't you? Flame,
flame, that is the start, you know, but it is not the
finish – that is still hidden. Water is the solution –
do you like my little joke? There is a reunion with
old friends, who so *very* want to pay their respects –
in person. Oh, see! There is a change of skin, sooner
than I had thought. And – one side makes things
smaller – and the other makes them larger. Take care
– it's when they're large, that is when their *teeth*
hurt most."

The Caterpillar sighed deeply. Then it
quickly turned away from them and started across
the cap, making its way nearly out of sight over its
vaulting, peaked crest.

"Wait – is that all?" the Knight cried.

Its soft voice floated back to them.

"Oh, no; it is never all. It is never lost, even
when the last breath is. Remember *that*, too. Yet I
think I understand what you are asking about; that's
simple. *He* dies, you know – *but then, again – so do
you.*"

The thing vanished from sight. A stunned
silence held them; they looked at one another.

"Well; it's good to know we're still on the *interesting* side of catastrophe," said the Knight.

"We should have stopped at 'hello'," the Knave replied.

After peering carefully about to be sure that the Caterpillar was no longer on its perch, the Knight went forward. She examined the toadstool from all sides and finally, she turned to Cass.

"One side still makes things smaller," she said.

"Humour me. How many sides does a circle have?" he asked.

"Exactly as many as Alice found; do you see? There are two different shades, one on this half circle, another on the back."

She returned to the monstrous fungus and spread her arms wide. Reaching as far as she could across a segment of the rim, Ava broke off two handfuls of cap. Cass joined her; each sample was indeed a different shade, one golden, the other a darker, russet hue.

"And which piece makes things larger – that's when the teeth hurt most?"

"Not sure how to tell; do you want to taste?" she asked.

"I don't need to know that badly. The situation itself, I hope, will answer the question. We should move." He was watching as shadows lengthened below the giant caps. Ava looked deep into the dark forest; leaves and twigs fell into a stifling silence. Other sounds came – the sound of clawed feet as they scratched softly across smooth sides of mushroom, and more distant, sobbing cries of pain.

Horrid place.

"Do we go through?" she asked.

But Cass had turned away from her; now he seemed to be listening to something. For a long moment, all Ava heard was the breeze, and the rustling of unknown things among the massive stalks. Then, far off – the sound of falling water.

It was not all.

She stopped then – now she heard it, too.

Hanging on the wind, what reached them was a chorus of many voices, a chorus that followed the sound of moving water, as it might trickle and play about a hidden source. It was an echo of words, repeated monotonously and horribly, rising and falling.

'She lies, we lie, She lies, we lie...'

The Knight and the Knave drew their weapons. Keeping a safe boundary between their heads and the gills of the mushroom caps, they made their way into the grove.

Ŧ

They left behind the musty, dry heaviness of the toadstool grove for the sound of falling water, a torrent's muted but thunderous roar.

Before them was a waterfall – a short distance away, water bubbled and foamed, cascading down the dark face of a high, sheer cliff. Above them, the sky was clear, cloudless – above the falls, rainbow mists and fogs rose, finding final form in a monumental tapestry of restless, surging clouds. Pewter-edged, the clouds coiled, churning high, their white peaks curling into the upper airs.

The flood of the falls emptied into a deep pool, which, in any normal world, would have been a place of peace and wondrous beauty. Wondrous it was. Green, it was, ringed on all sides with more green, in every hue and texture, from the tall, golden-crested reeds, to lily pads on the water's calm surface, to the delicate gossamer grasses whose heads nodded in the wind. At the foot of the falls, the turbulent water bubbled and foamed, slowing to rippling eddies at the pool's rock strewn, mossy perimeter. Scattered amongst the tall grasses, lilies abounded. Large, they were, so large at this distance that they could be nothing less than giants. Their wide petals, orange and red, and splashed with dark stripes and spots, swayed eerily, and strange sounds carried back on the wind.

"Like tigers growling," said Cass. "And they're moving against the wind."

"If those are the Tiger Lilies, I think we may have found the rest of the teeth."

Cass looked up: under the clear blue sky away from the torrent, here birds should have been plentiful – here, there were none.

Yet life – rich, unpredictable, dangerous – flourishes still.

It thrives in terrible aberrance, violent and strange.

The Knave and the Knight picked their way between the beds, seeking the source of the grotesque litany that had called them from the mushroom forest.

Before them spread an enormous field.

Ranging in long, meticulously groomed rows, Sun Flowers crowded the field – their petals stretched more than a foot long. The heavy seed heads swayed in the breeze, and each flower face, densely packed with seeds, spanned nearly a meter.

The visitors drew near. Row upon row, the chest- high showy giants were planted right up to the path, and the closest flower heads were soon before them. Without a word, Cass and Ava halted where they stood, transfixed by a ghastly spectacle.

The seed kernels themselves were massive.

Each of the seeds was the size of the Knight's closed fist – and every one of them, on every single plant in the acres- wide field – every one of them bore the image of a living human face.

Chapter 20

TORNSOULS

The low, plaintive cries of countless voices filled the air.

Tormented whispers, the dreary tales of monotonous and never –ending captivity – and the soul-wrenching cries for mercy, for release – all battered the ears of the watchers, until they steeled themselves just to remain where they were.

Infinitely horrible now rose and fell the doleful refrain – *She lies, we lie, She lies, we lie....*

Cass' jaw stiffened.

"I swear. I swear I will bring Her down."

At his words, the Sun Flower heads ceased their chant; slowly all the massive flower heads turned toward them.

"Why do you lie?" the Knight asked.

For a moment the litany faltered; the eyes of those seed faces closest to them blinked – the terrible anguish was replaced by a multitude of gazes – of bright wonder, confusion, doubt – and even greater fear.

243

'We cannot say, we must not say, we cannot say....'

The Knave moved forward; the Knight followed. In one of the seed faces before them, there was a visage of horror and poignant despair.

The two gathered close beside the Sun Flower; there in one of the kernels was indeed the face of the Duke and the slain man's eyes sought theirs, searching, pleading.

"My Knight – my Knave," said the murdered man.

"Your Grace, we came too late," said the Knight sadly.

From the Duke's face in the seed came a wail; soon it changed again to his low voice, barely above a whisper.

"I bear you no ill will. Not even the wise can see all ends. I was coming to find you, to warn you. *She...*"

Tears filled the Duke's eyes. The Knight answered softly. "We have already encountered .... *Her.*"

The Duke's eyes widened horribly. "And you stand here – yet alive? Woe, alas!"

"How so, Sir?"

"Perhaps an easy death would prove a blessing. For you to be yet alive – there is a terrible purpose there. Does She mean to play at you, like a cat plays a mouse, to torment you before the end, before the final dice are thrown?"

Ava scowled. "Games, again."

"Perhaps – it is not just a game," came the dreadful whisper. "You will have to be bold, reckless. Are you prepared? Do you dare? *To catch Her – you will have to risk all.*"

The young woman did not reply; a dark look overspread her face.

Brighter than the sun, more dismal than the grave, the long lines of yellow flowers spread into the distance.

"They lie," Cass warned the Knight.

"Alas, yes!" cried the Duke. "They are bound to, they must. They have been here long. Not I! Speak softly, so that you do not add your voice to ours!"

"My Lord, who are all these?" exclaimed the Knight.

A bitter look came into the dead man's eyes.

"All that have fallen before *Her.* The Hatter has not yet come to share our sorrow – but there is little time remaining, you do not know how weak he has become – soon he, too, must fall! And, if so, if he falls while still enchained – all hope is lost. For him. For all."

"Lost?" demanded the Mage.

The Duke's face took on a look of pure terror.

"Soft! For your life: Soft! Aye – lost to peace, to rest, to mercy. Alas for all – for will She then be strong enough – to rise? *To pass ....Above?* Who will prevent Her, then?"

His eyes roved, searching their faces, seeking the freedom of land and sky above – all beyond his reach.

"*To rise?* Cass, they know! Look at them, look at him, think how much he knows," Ava cried. "If we can only learn how!"

Voices, low and terrible, again rose from the field of the cursed.

'We lie, She lies, we lie, She lies...'

"But *you* – do not," the Mage said, and he fixed his eyes again on those of the Duke. "Can we save him? Can you tell us how?"

A deep groan came from the Duke. The captive man's lips trembled as he sought to speak. Desperately, he tried to answer them; tried and failed, and the look of pain spread, from his own face to those of the seed faces nearest his.

"I cannot," he whispered. "*She* is too strong."

Eagerly, Ava pulled Cass back, away from the field of torment.

"He may be our only hope," she said. "We must learn how to stop Her. Force him to tell us — *Command him to speak.*"

The Knave stared at the one bereft of hope, beyond the reach of peace.

"What if it kills him?"

Ava looked back to the soul fettered there in the flower's seed.

"He's already dead."

"Not here," Cass replied.

"*Look at him.* Is that life? If that were *me*, there in that seed — what would you do? Would you give me peace? *Would you save me, Cass?*"

He cast a dreadful look upon her.

The Mage stepped forward. At first, there was only his still form, standing there, his eyes fixed on the Duke. Then, suddenly a pale glow became manifest about the body of the Sorcercr.

Ava stared at him; again, she felt the touch of fear.

The man's arm came slowly up, extended, with his hand palm down – iridescent light coursed along that limb, becoming stronger and brighter. Light was everywhere, from his fingertips to the young Mage's face, upon whose forehead a richer and brighter glow found its heart as the quincunx formed. The light became blinding and Ava saw another face, older, different, one that melded with the features of the one before her.

I know that face.

That is the face I saw on the hill; that is the face of the One at the altar stone.

The Mage's hand turned palm upward and he spoke, not only in the voice of the Knave, but in the tones of the *other* as moment by moment, the man before her grew less and less recognisable.

"I Command Thee."

His voice resounded.

Like a shock wave, light rose from the Mage and rolled like a tide across the field of the damned.

All the seed faces in the field turned toward the Mage, even as did that of the Duke. The morbid litany ceased utterly for a heartbeat – then it began to change as each voice, one by one across the field, took up the new chant.

'We hear, She hears, we hear, She hears ...'

The Duke's face contorted madly and he shouted above the rising din.

"Stop! *She* hears! Find the way, turn the Key!"

Rising from the cursed soil itself, a bestial snarl drowned out his voice.

All at once, explosive arcs of blue light played over the field of woe. Each face in each seed cried out and the pool below the cascade rippled and surged, its waves foaming and cresting over the emerald banks.

Above the Mage, lightning flickered white-hot across the sky. It pierced the clouds that now rose like angry monoliths, churning higher above the falls. The eyes of each seed face turned, turned until the gaze of all was directed in one line – and within the eyes of each seed face, one after another – darkness opened, spreading until it filled each seed.

The black void lasted only a second.

In the next instant, the shadows dissolved, lifting from each seed. Replacing the shadows, another face grew, larger and larger, into greater and more terrible clarity until the face of the Black Queen glared out from every one of the seeds.

All except one.

Alone in the field of the possessed, the seed face of the Duke still bore the features of the slain man. That face twisted in wrenching pain and a nightmarish scream rang across the field.

Yet in the final moment, with his last and most piteous sigh – his eyes shone out. Not with fear, nor even with pain, the eyes of the man She had killed now filled once more with tears. A wondrous smile lit the softened features.

"No more! No more of pain, of fear, of living death. With strength, with courage – comes freedom. *She* cannot touch me now. Free! I am free! Thou hast saved me! Come – come forward, Mage, come near."

The Mage bent over the bloom; a soft whisper arose from the seed bearing the face of the fallen man and Cass nodded. Then, a look of unutterable joy and peace came over his face, and then – he was gone.

Like so many dreadful mirrors across the field, the face of his tormentor blanched with hate and fury, for the Queen could no longer touch him. The Duke had passed beyond her desolating reach.

Taken up as dim, resonant echoes by the ones in the field, the voice of the Black Queen radiated from the seed head closest to them.

"You cannot win."

"I do not have to win to vanquish you," the Mage replied.

Her eyes blazed cold and black with triumph.

"How sweetly you reveal your purpose. How tenderly you betray *her* trust! Who dies – at whose hands? Roll the dice with me, Mage! Roll the dice and see. Who will pay the price for your arrogance? For you are arrogant, Mage, you grow more so with each trial, with each ascent to power."

Bright and sharp as obsidian edged razors, Her gaze flicked to the Knight.

"Your Knight knows, does she not? Your Knight – but for how much longer? *Look at her!* See how her fear grows! And fear is ever the willing hand – it wields the sword of desperate action. You will lose all. Whom do you cherish? *What are you prepared to lose?* Life? Soul? Either or both – and I win. Consider the price of losing. You will remain with me. You will be mine. Here have I held sway for many lifetimes. Those who stood against me are now my slaves."

"Not the Hatter," Cass said. "Not yet."

A low growl came from the seed head.

But the Mage looked now to his Knight, who flung her drawn sword to his hand. The moment the Mage's hand grasped the hilt, the blade's bright edge grew brighter still, as if honed with lightning. In one sweeping pass, he sheared off the entire head of the cursed bloom that bore the monarch's face.

It landed heavily at their feet, rolling and finally coming to rest. Now every seed in the terrible head stared up at the sky. Slowly, all the seed faces grew darker and darker, and the face of the Queen dissolved away. Yet no other faces came to claim the place of Her image. The Sun Flower's seeds were once more merely seeds.

But from the field, from the lines and masses of flowers that remained, whose seed faces once more regained their captive state, a soft and terrible chant was in the suddenly frigid air.

'She dies, we die, She dies, we die…'

The Mage faced the Knight.

He turned the sword in his hand; a line of dark blood marked the edge of the naked blade. Then, he took hold of the blade – and offered the sword to the Knight, hilts first.

Pale light still flickered along the weapon's edge. For a moment, the sharp tip of the sword pointed back at the Sorcerer – aimed directly at his heart.

The Knight's eyes stayed long on his. Slowly, she took the sword, sheathed it. She turned and started away, away from the field as Cass looked once more at the giant flower head on the ground.

Silent it is.

Dead and still; a token of victory – and a warning.

He looked at the stain of blood on his palm. Then he followed the Knight; he did not look back.

He did not see how, from deep within the falls, with its clouds shifting tumultuously above – two eyes, brightly bathed by the icy stream – had finally turned away from the spectacle in the field,

to disappear within the torrent's never-ending flow.

Chapter 21

MASTER

"I am not."

"You are."

The Knight set a furious pace away from the garden, away from him. She held aside a branch that flew back to catch him squarely in the face, raising a stinging welt.

The Knight was well ahead of him when his head cleared. He raced forward.

"Ava. Ava – wait!"

Taking her arm, he dragged her to a stop, forcing her to face him.

"She saw it."

"*She* lies!"

"Not in this!"

She fought his grip; he tightened it.

"You might be strong enough to get away; then again, maybe not."

"Do you want to test that?" she growled. Her eyes fixed on his face, and the look in them was terrible.

"Fitz! It's me – it's just me."

"'Just you'? Is it? It wasn't five minutes ago."

He let her go. She pulled away; then she stalked back to him, her hand rising, to stop at the point of his chest where he had aimed her own sword's point.

"Each time. Each time you do this, Cass – I look at you, and I'm less and less sure – is it still you? *Someone else is there, just beneath the surface. Something else is there.* I don't know what that thing is. What it will do – what it can do."

He stared at her. In his head were the half-remembered bits of a fateful poem, one whose verses could be ascribed more and more – to him, and to here. With face still flushed from the ordeal at the field, he turned away from the Knight, lost in her words and the fear they had called up.

'Weave a circle round him thrice, and close your eyes with holy dread.

For he on honeydew hath fed – and drunk the milk of Paradise…'

How could I tell her? How can I tell her how it is each time – how intoxicating, how overwhelming – how with each time, with each new

256

sortie into that realm, so exotic, so sensual – it has
changed me? In spirit, in essence, in ways I cannot
explain or describe. Sorcery – it flows, over me; now,
through me, like a tide. As irresistible as the needs of
the flesh, calling me – and with each calling – serves.

He spoke aloud then, but so softly, that the
Knight was hardly certain that she had heard.

"Will I ever be able to feel that way again –
anywhere but here?"

He looked back to see the Knight was staring
at him. He took a step toward her, only to see her
step back.

"My Knight; I would never hurt you," said
the Mage.

"My Lord, would you even know if you had?
When you're there – in that place – do any of us
exist? Do I still exist for you – as human? *Think,*
Cass. What could you not do? What would you not
do, now? You should never have come here; I never
wanted you to be here, not like this."

"I had to! You know why, you saw why…"

A low inarticulate cry came from her.

"Is that why? Is that really why you came?"

He ran to her, taking up both her hands in his.

"Listen to me. Can you beat *Her*? Can you take Her alone, Fitz? *Can we do this without – what I do?* Do I stop now, do I give it up, I can, I can change my skin; the Rabbit said so! What would you have me be, what shall I become – to do what I must?"

She pulled her hands free and stepped away, her hand raised.

"Stop! Stop .. where you are. What if it's not the skin, Cass – what if it's what you always were? What if – deep inside you – this was always there?"

His hands reached toward hers. Now he looked down at them. They were empty, the long fingers spread wide, reaching, reaching.

Empty.

His own hands, true – yet foreign in some way, and once more his voice was such that the girl could barely catch his words.

"If this is meant to be – what part of myself must I give up, then?"

Tears filled the Knight's eyes.

"*What are you prepared to lose?* What part of you – am *I* prepared to lose? None of you, Cass. None of you."

Her voice broke.

Before she could move, the Mage was before her.

He pulled her against him. His arms were tight around her, his hands in her hair, over her lips. He kissed her, savagely, desperately, unmindful of anything but need and desire, blind and insistent.

For a moment, there was nothing but the warmth of her in his arms, the yielding pressure of her body against his, and the hunger in her that matched his own.

For a moment, a world – one of terrible wonder, one filled with marvel, yet one whose very fabric was interwoven with uncompromising violence and certain death – went utterly away, and for the first time, he was content with it.

"You are doing it all wrong,"

The voice was very soft, very low, and came from somewhere in the tall grass not twenty paces from their feet. The Knight and the Mage started.

"I thought it was going quite well," the Mage murmured.

He did not fully release his hold upon Ava, even as the grass rustled, and the unseen speaker went on.

"It takes all the holding you can do to get to the next place. So you must hold her far more tightly," came the wry advice. "That way, she won't be able to get away. Then you will always know where she is."

"Where is that?" Cass asked, craning his neck to catch sight of the hidden one, finally loosening his hold on the Knight and positioning himself in front of her.

"Why, in your arms, of course! Here, with you, with all of us, *always* – now, won't that be nice?"

Recoiling in horror from this very idea, the Mage stepped away from the Knight as if she had suddenly taken on the attributes of a white-hot poker and both drew their swords.

The grass swayed. The speaker rose into view. Then, it stood up on its round, fat hindquarters, carefully removing with one supple paw a few dead leaves from its smooth, brown pelt. It was a fairly large creature.

Cass stared at the thing. "Wombat?"

"No; considering where we are, something much more dangerous. Dormouse," Ava murmured. "Very*... large...* Dormouse."

The Dormouse waddled toward them and came to a respectful halt several paces away. It settled back onto its haunches and yawned widely, meticulously grooming its long whiskers before addressing them again. Its eyes sparkled hopefully.

"Will there be any more today?" it asked.

"No!" Ava insisted.

"Not today," the Mage added, but his glance at the Knight made her face flush again, even while she glared at him.

The Dormouse chuckled.

"You mustn't frown so. First – it does no good regretting things that have already taken upon themselves the trouble of happening. Second — it makes one look peevish. Well then, if you are ready, or even if you are not, you should go on, down the path. It's all right, it's quite as safe as any other path

261

here. Which is to say… well, *you* know by now, don't you?"

The fuzzy creature turned its head towards a heavily overgrown trail that led into the wood beyond the glade.

"He will be there, you know," continued the oversized rodent. "At the *end* – there's a joke there somewhere. I will let you know when I find it. But, do hurry now, if you can – the storm is coming."

The Dormouse regarded them with a strange glitter in its eyes. It suddenly turned and waddled away, disappearing with a soft rustle into a thicket.

"Will she be there, too?" the Mage wondered.

"I hope not," said the Knight.

"I meant *Alice* …"

Without another word, he walked past her and started down the path.

Ŧ

The way was so thickly overgrown with tall grass and saplings that Cass wondered when it might ever have been used freely.

*If this is the way, he has been nearly walled
in here, like silk trammels up the prey of some
cunning and voracious spider.*

*What is so special about this place – so close
to him – that this has happened?*

They were brought to a halt by a large bush
directly in their patch, and the Mage hacked at it
with his sword.

The sap flowed freely from the severed stems,
the green fluid marking the edge of the Mage's
blade.

A dreadful sigh rose up; it came from the
heart of the thick mass of remaining stems. Like the
soft wail of a dying child, the sound floated for a
moment on the wind. Then, it faded away, and with
its loss, as the Knight and the Mage watched, what
had been a tall, vigorous growing thing began to
droop before their eyes. In seconds, its leaves had
curled and died before them.

Chilled by the sight, and eager to leave this
place, Cass raised his sword again – green no longer
was the sap that had stained the weapon's length.

Now the blade was crimson with the sheen of
fast drying blood.

Sounds came from just ahead – the clatter of dishes and cups and, all too near – a strange, alarming hissing sound that halted abruptly as if the maker had grown suddenly aware of them.

The Mage and the Knight cut their way through the last tangle of weeds and shrubs to reach a clearing; they stepped out onto a meadow of well-shorn grass, with a tall, imposing house set at its far end.

"Hold," came the Knight's whisper.

Draped in fine linen and set with cups, plates and assorted tea pots, a long table stood at the centre of the vale.

Scattered in the grass before the table, the bleached bones of small animals lay.

Some of the bits seemed very old, and on many, the deep marks of sharp teeth could be seen. There was a slight movement at the edge of the drape nearest the ground. There the Dormouse appeared suddenly, scuttling out from beneath the table. The Dormouse sniffed over the pile of bones, then it selected a long, thin remnant from the pile in the grass. It turned and promptly vanished again with the morsel behind the tablecloth, from which crunching sounds came.

Cups clattered noisily, and high, cracking laughter pealed out. It came from the thing seated on a chair at the table's end – a Hare.

"He's almost as tall as I am," Ava said.

Covered in patchy grey and white fur and sporting waistcoat and breeches and a single glove, all as tattered and threadbare as the Rabbit's, the Hare laughed again. The sound was chilling; it was the laugh of one whose mind had splintered long ago. The creature turned to face them.

Keen and cunning yet alienated from all sense were the yellow eyes that gleamed from the beast in the chair.

The mad thing smiled.

Its right paw was bare. The Hare raised that paw, with its long, fingerlike claws and hideous cracked talons to direct their gaze toward the stooped figure seated on its right.

"My God," the Knight. "It's him."

Chapter 22

IT'S MY PARTY

"Approach, friends – admirers! Don't be shy!" the Hare cried in a tinny, rasping voice.

The creature watched them as they came near the table. It watched them, as though the swords in their hands were utterly without significance, as if their bones would soon be added to the sorry remains littering the grass.

It was all the Knight could do – to walk calmly toward the madness before them, to keep herself from running headlong to the table, to the bent figure of the man beside the Hare. That one finally raised his head and his eyes met theirs.

"Allow me to introduce – my Hatter," said the Hare. "He doesn't say much – not anymore – but he amuses us no end!"

There was a feral gleam in the Hare's eyes as he regarded the man beside him. One of the Hatter's pale hands remained poised in air, teaspoon quivering, as he stared at the visitors, looking from the Knight to the Knave. His gaze looked beyond the

Knave's festive garments as if the Hatter suddenly perceived the identity of the one before him; there came a sharp intake of the Hatter's breath.

"Good, sir. We have come a great way to find you," the Knight said.

The Hatter made no answer. Without warning, the Hare's long arm shot out and he cuffed the Hatter sharply on the ear.

"Speak, Pig! We have guests!" he hissed.

"Leave off," growled the Knave to the creature with chaos in its eyes. Those eyes widened but the Hare made no more attempts to touch the Hatter; it laughed.

"Offer them some tea!" the Hare urged.

"My boy – will you and your Knight honour an old man with your presence?" the Hatter asked.

The Hare glowered. It shot a quick glance at the Hatter, at the tremble in the man's hands and head that finally loosened a lock of the once dark hair. The look of deep suspicion on its whiskered face grew, quickly changing to rage. The Hare gnashed its sharp teeth when Cass suddenly took the empty chair opposite their host and sat down, setting his sword on the table, with its hilts beside his hand.

The Knight took a seat beside her companion and did likewise.

As such, the two swords – on one side and the other – held within their razor edges the one who had been Carroll. Walled away from the Hare, there he sat, bastioned by steel forged with iron, harboured within two ramparts of tempered death.

The Hare realised this – with a great cry, it jumped up onto its feet. With its paws clenched tightly, the animal quivered with hate and anger.

Happily would it have rent the man at the table, but its lightning reach with its claws drew a rippling arc of angry sparks the moment its ragged talons approached the sword lengths and the man girt by iron on either side.

Helplessly, the vicious thing turned baleful eyes on the hunched figure with its shabby suit, soiled and unbuttoned collar, and sad, patch- worked tie. Then it glared at the Knight and the Knave.

"You! You think to stymie me, to thwart us all! Think again. He will not leave with you! His time allotted is not yet spent – when it is, fall he must, as have all the others. Did you not know? *The Creator lives only as long as the Created – look at*

*him. A sorry, cursed mess. He visualised a Queen –
and see what a marvelous creature has come from
that! He is now Her favourite plaything – She will
not part with him."*

The Hare shook a long, claw-tipped finger at
them.

*"You, Knight! You, who would ascend – will
it be to a throne? Hark! Once won – Her place will
not long be held by you! And you – Knave – no one
can save you – your Trial comes soon. You wondered
about the doors, the doors in the hall, in the castle –
there are doors everywhere! Are you brave enough –
or foolish enough, to open them? Which will you
open? What will you find – salvation—or will you
find Her claws at your throat?"*

The Hare spat at the man he could not touch,
then it grinned wickedly.

"You pity him, do you? Save yourself the
trouble. This old man – he is not what he seems. Did
you really believe all those marks on the bones
below – were the work of the Dormouse?"

The mad creature gave a harsh, high laugh.
Then it spun away from the table and, dropping

horribly to all fours, the Hare bounded away from them, to disappear into the forest behind the house.

Rising from the table in horror, both Knight and Knave stared after the thing as it vanished from sight.

A piteous sigh drew their eyes down to their host.

Hair strewn in disarray, with his white hands still clutching the naked blades and with tears on his pale cheeks, the spirit of the man who had been Lewis Carroll had finally sprawled, face down and senseless upon the smooth, white tablecloth.

Ŧ

The liquor from the Knight's flask had brought colour back to the Hatter's cheeks after his guests had pulled him from the table and laid him upon the grass.

Now, warmed by sun, made vigorous by their care, he sat and looked about him, as if seeing the place – the meadow, the relentlessly endless table settings, the grim house in the background – for the first time.

They helped him rise. The house was as worn as he, with its doors and thatch marred and spent. And under its pristine cloth, the tea table's legs were shifting and splitting with age.

With age and more; some force, one that lent an evil twist to all circumstances, one that worked to corrupt and undermine the natural growth and life of all healthy things – was at work here.

It was just as they had seen elsewhere.

After fortifying the Hatter with wine and cake, they waited for him to regain strength and sense enough to speak. Soon the man's eyes were no longer dim, now his voice rang strong and clear in the meadow, even as he strove to keep his tones low. The Knight did not wonder at this.

What else is here – listening – so that She may know, too?

She listened now as the Hatter replied to the Mage.

"I never dreamt I would ever experience non-Euclidean geometry – I simply never believed in it. So much the worse for me; I was a poor mathematician, and an even worse logician," he said sadly.

"Nonsense," the Mage demurred. "Your paradox work is studied even today."

Genuine gratitude lit the captive man's face, yet his voice faltered once more. "Paradox! Ah, yes; and who knew how that would reckon? But I am grieved to see you here, in this dreadful place. I was a fool to involve anyone else in this, even as a deathbed promise. The Hare spoke truly, you know. 'You will leave when I do,' that is what *She* said. She torments me. She will never let me go. And in this Under world, it is still too strong - this *thing*."

The Mage regarded him closely and the Knight was amazed at his reply.

"This 'nexus'?"

Again, the Hatter's eyes grew bright. "Yes! An *excellent* word! This nexus, as you call it – it feeds on the ether force of a man, of a life."

The Sorcerer studied him but what he thought – about the identity of the Queen, his growing suspicions about her kingdom and the space around them – he did not disclose to the one before them.

"You mean energy," offered the Mage.

273

"Yes. I did give it a basis, a form, an inner life; my thoughts did. It was an accident, when I stumbled into that hole – but it started the moment I came here. It fed upon me, even as I fed upon it."

The Knight studied him gravely.

"You couldn't stop."

He sighed again. "Soon, my dear, I had no choice. I was caught – as you may be yourselves. You have brought new voices, stronger and even more vivid than mine. God help you! I feel that, very soon, *She* will have no more need of me, now that *you* have come."

That drew silence from them.

"Then, you don't actually know how to bring Her down?" Cass asked.

The Hatter did not answer immediately; instead, his voice grew dreamy and distant.

"Once, perhaps. Once, long, long ago, I knew or at least I suspected. So close we were – how much closer now? So many strange things have happened – just recently, indeed, just before you entered the nexus, as you say. It was as though something had changed, something integral and important had come into it. I cannot say what it will mean. Yet this

I know – that *you*, with your new symbols, the new strength and weakness within you – you have altered the initial premises of the paradox here. For, there is one, still potent, still very dangerous and real."

"And the child? What of Alice?" Ava asked, softly.

A look of pain crossed his face. He seemed suddenly frailer, even more distant than before and his voice grew weaker. The sun passed behind a cloud and the old house behind him seemed somehow less substantial, masked by shadow.

"*Her Spirit is freed, when I am*. The rules here have changed," the Hatter replied. "Yet, I cannot tell you how – 'I can't go back to yesterday, I was a different person then'. Yet, I sense – if you change the premise, *if you change the premise…* Find the operative word, my good fellow; re-define it!"

Cass frowned. "At the moment, the operative word, Sir, is *'leave.'*

A look of dread passed over the man's features, eternally young, yet old and his voice altered.

"That may change – to a word more powerful, more devastating – to you, and to us all. Be prepared. I felt it in my heart. I am powerless here, but *you* – what are *you* prepared to do, young man, to make it so?"

A queer wind began to rise; they could hear its voice as it murmured mournfully around the house at the edge of the meadow. In fear, the Hatter looked up into the clouds that had begun to gather overhead; his voice was urgent with haste, his words terrifying.

'Long, long ago it passed from Him,
To me, and then to her.
'Tis Power's way to sleep
'Till waked, by fate and character.

The way will close, then open be.
The riddle here is plain:
Thou hast but One, but there are Two,
'Tis she who holds the Twain!

A prison dark, a woman's tears,
From hate will come a friend.

First large, then small,
Yet size is All!
And Fire speeds the End!

Yet 'ware Her Voice!
Her smile, Her hand.
An offer – Not a choice!
From sleeping – Wake!
With Water – Take
Thy Love from Under Land.'

Blown by the rising wind, leaves blew madly across the meadow, and a look of terror fixed itself on the Hatter's pale features.

"She calls! Hurry! Get away! The Door! Find the Door – to *Her* it leads, but also to escape! *The Key comes!*"

The gust rose to a small but perfect gale. It buffeted the Hatter, tearing at his clothes, his hair, his very form, and he winced in pain.

The wind howled. From deep within it, savage and insistent voices moaned, and the talons of dark claws loomed in and out of sight in the cyclone's winds. The Hatter's voice was lost, now one with the chorus of wails carried on the merciless airs that suddenly surrounded him. Caught, the man struggled as the claws in the wind tore at him, drawing him deep within the heart of the cyclone, finally obscuring him completely.

Swords useless in their trembling hands, his saviours stood helpless – when the winds at last died away, the table was empty.

The meadow stretched before them, deserted save for their own shaken presence. Yet the Hatter – the man they had come to save, the spirit that was Lewis Carroll – was gone.

Chapter 23

FIRE

Cass heard a sharp intake of breath beside him.

The Knight was staring at the house, where, from the curtained window beside the shut front door – something – white, and hurried and accompanied by a gleam of eyes had appeared and promptly vanished.

Untouched by the wind and fury the house stood waiting on its small hill beside the meadow. They drew near and ascended the stone porch, before the door they halted.

"Doors," murmured Cass. "The Hare spoke of more doors."

With the point of her blade, the Knight thrust at the door. It slowly moved inward, opening to them a darkly shadowed space. This time, it was the Mage who barred the way – he kept Ava outside, behind him as he cautiously stepped across the threshold.

Musty, like the smell of an old attic.
Disused, yet somehow full – of memories.

And what else?

At his nod, the Knight entered and they stood side by side in a hallway, silent and dark. When the door closed behind them under its own power, the two jumped. The Mage turned and faced the door; when he reached for the brass knob, the door opened, feeding itself into his hand freely.

"Convenient. If I could train my own doors to do this – well, at least we might be able to get out."

They made their way down a long hallway, shadowed but for the scattered bits of light that found their way past the old faded curtains at the front of the house. A low sound drew them into a large sitting room, with sofas and over- stuffed chairs scattered about. Portraits lined the walls; with their subjects' faces solemn and grave and eyes that looked down dourly at the visitors. The Knight and the Knave circled the room, stopping before a large fireplace, within whose massive grate a fire burned brightly. It did little to relieve the sense of dismal vacancy and somberness permeating the place.

"He mentioned fire," the Knight said. "Is this what he meant?"

"No," replied her companion. "Although I can't tell you why."

Sitting on the wide marble mantel and held within a gilded frame, an enormous mirror silvered with age was set. Before it, a massive painting had been propped. From its ancient surface, dark with grime and smoke, the dim features of a once-lovely woman peered out. Cass gasped and the Knight drew near; the Mage was intently studying the carved stone pillars that supported the heavy mantel.

The likeness of a woman's face was also there, carved in the stone.

"It's the face of the Red Queen, the Queen of Hearts, as it is on the card," Ava said.

"No. Look," he replied.

It was true – before their eyes, the stony visage had begun to change. Pale mist hovered over the face, whose lines and lineaments slowly altered until a different face, not unfamiliar, took form – with its proud neck and full lips – the face of the Black Queen now found its form in the living stone.

On the mantel, the portrait had also stirred into awful life. Cass drew near, now he stood motionless before the portrait whose features, clouded by cold mist, came slowly but surely to mimic those of his enemy. The crackling of the fire below, the voice of the Knight as she called to him – all these sounds grew muted. A great stillness descended, flowing through him like the grip of a chill fever.

He, alone, in his mind, heard the voice of the Queen, low and captivating.

"No fear, now. No more fear," he replied.

"Cass!" It was Ava; she was gripping his arm, she was pulling at him, yanking him with all her strength until she turned him, away from the portrait with its sweet smile, and welcoming lips. Now the Mage faced her completely. He seemed calm and focused, but she could only imagine what had passed between them as he had faced his nemesis. Now the Knight turned the portrait, reversing it, facing it into the mirror that loomed over the mantel. The girl stood before the Mage.

"A little fear is a good thing," she said, her eyes going once more to the portrait, as though she would have liked to hurl it into the fire burning below.

"What happened? Did She speak to you?" the Knight continued.

"No," he answered calmly. "There was nothing at all."

Yet the Dark Lady's words were still in his mind, even as he spoke the lie.

Beware.

The Knight – Beware.

Beware the Knight.

They stepped back, for without warning – the flames in the grate rose up in a flurry of violent heat and brilliance. A storm of cinders flew upward into the chimney as a great log, its heart glowing with living fire, split apart. A thick piece of the log, still smoldering, rolled into the room itself. There it splintered again into hot embers, and from the heart of the largest coal – a form appeared.

Vibrantly alive, apparently at one with its fiery home, with short tail lashing, it scurried across the floor. Colour – a stunning array of bright red, yellow and black spots covered the creature's form, which was gun metal grey and as moist as if it had just emerged from a pond's green coolness.

"Alive in the flames," breathed the Knight.

"Yes. *Salamander....salamander*," he replied.

At his words, the anomaly looked up directly at him, its eyes glistening. Then it scuttled away, passing through the door into the hallway, making for the stairs.

Cass looked once more at the portrait's back, its dreadful face turned in against the mirror; he turned to the Knight.

"Come on – it's up there somewhere." The two left the sitting room; they halted in the stairwell, their eyes directed upward to the dark landing above.

They left behind them a room empty but not vacant. For upon the heels of their departure, a dreadful change was taking place. Angrily, sending flaming cinders high, the fire in the grate surged again upward into life – then the flames dwindled, falling lower and lower until only the barest glow of light escaped into the sad room. In that room, from every corner, shadows crept, their darkness spreading across the faded carpets and dusty parquet.

Still the fire struggled against the dark, sending one more bright flame upward; then it lapsed again into mere coals. Yet, above the mantel, light of a different sort had awakened and now held sway.

In its gilt frame, the mirror's surface began to shimmer. Like a flood of water streaming and flowing over the glass, the mirror's surface was now awash in light. Ripples of silver, forming into sheer fabric like spun moonlight, turned, turned in the frame until robes took form, and the wearer herself looked out once again into the room.

Shadows filled the sitting room and in the mirror behind the turned portrait, the regal throat and face and eyes of the Black Queen shone out – those eyes burned blackly as she fixed upon the Knight – and the Sorcerer – as they started up the darkened stairwell, ascending the stairs.

The landing they reached was grim and dark, the hallway long – it did not conceal the flash of red and black, moist and swiftly moving along the floor ahead. From the darkness of the corridor, they heard the soft click of a door closing.

Yet, which one? Door after door lined the hall's length, door after door and all of them closed. Cass went to the first he saw; the door opened easily to his hand. Yet he remained where he stood, then drew the door closed as Ava joined him.

"Shouldn't we go in?"

"No," he replied. "It's not the right door."

"How do you know that?'

"Because it opened," he said.

He continued down the hall, opening and closing doors until he came to the last. Alone amongst them all – this was one whose knob did not yield to the Sorcerer's grip. With the Knight at his side, he studied the door, with its simple wood, its frame of peeling paint. The Mage put his bare hand flat upon it.

"No," Ava said. "Don't."

"Why not?" Cass asked.

A strange look came over the Knight.

"I'm afraid," she replied softly. "Afraid, as I have never been before. I'm afraid, Cass – and I don't know why. *Is She behind that door?* Is this the door with the claws on the other side – Her claws, reaching for your throat? Let's leave this house."

'No!" he exclaimed. His face was flushed; the wild gleam in his eye and his vehemence startled the girl at his side.

"Do you want to die?" she demanded.

"No. No more than you do."

The Knight stepped back, distraught.

"Is this what *She* said to you, downstairs? That if you came readily – willingly – to Her – that She would spare you?"

"Ava – stop. You know that's nonsense!"

"Do I? Don't you see? Do you not see – in the dell – those arrows? Those arrows were not meant for you – they were meant for me! *I am in Her way – then – and now!*"

With that, she drew her sword and pointed it straight at his throat.

Time stopped.

The Mage looked at his Knight, his eyes and face terrible to behold. For the space of a heartbeat, the girl saw on his finger a ring of bright gold; it flashed in the darkness, shining on a finger that had been bare before. Then all was dark again, dark and still, deathly silent – as though the eyes of the house – and more, were upon them both. The Sorcerer's voice was low in the hallway.

"There is none other for me – than you."

Her face went white – the Knight lowered her sword to the sound of a soft click – and the door before them slowly opened inward.

Within the room – if room it was – all was dark, and into darkness the Sorcerer turned, and stepped – and vanished.

Chapter 24

LĒOHT

It was silent as a tomb except for the muted sound of the Mage's boots.

He slowly walked across what should have been just the floor of just another room in the Hatter's house – and was instead pine needles, sere, deep, heavy with scent.

The throbbing in his head had subsided. His vision had cleared enough to reveal that he walked in a dark wood, not unlike the pine glade where the Duke and nearly they themselves had found bloody death.

A dark wood.

What appears to be a dark wood.

But where are You?

The trees were mere silhouettes against a star filled sky. But yet he saw it, there in the tall tree across the way, there was what he had sought, seemingly since he had first ventured up onto the Mount, in search of answers, discovering instead a mangled fox.

289

Discovering the beginning of all – this.

The dark form of the hawk was enormous, its head stark against the stars and for a second, the Mage imagined a crown, glittering and cold and white surmounting the bird's head. Pale blue light shone on the ground before him; when he looked back to the tree – the raptor was gone.

Instead, on the ground below the tree, the One he sought had appeared.

He was not tall, even as Ava had described Him so long ago to Abby – and even here, His cloak and robes were coarsely woven. But the man with the diadem on His brow smiled in the gloom of this enchanted space; His smile was for the young man who waited as the Master made His way forward, a simple yew staff in His youthful grip.

He halted before Cass; the dark gaze of one returned by the blue gaze of the other. Master and Mage cautiously took in one another. Then the Master, the Wizard – smiled again.

"Did you think I was taller, too? You don't seem at all surprised to see me," He said, His voice rich and low. "That's good."

"I've seen every evidence of You – Your presence, Your power, Your touch – since the beginning. I just didn't see it clearly," Cass said.

"Tell me, Caspian Hythe – what did you see?" asked the Wizard.

"Up on the Mount, I heard Your voice – and the fox was there at my feet. Did You send Gryphon to leave it there?'

"No. The Gryphon is not My creature. We'd chatted of course, but he is what he is, and he does what he does – in whatever world he finds himself, including the upper ones."

Cass nodded. "Then, the portal – in hindsight, there had to be something as powerful as She at work – something perhaps, more powerful?"

The Wizard laughed. "More powerful – we shall see. But, *good* – and, then?"

"Oh, the Undine and the first card, the urge to pull that card, dare I say – the 'command' to do so?"

The Wizard settled himself on a large boulder.

"To summon an Elemental is not easy – the first time, it's nearly impossible; I did help. It will get easier, I promise."

"Easier?" The Mage looked wonderingly at the Master before continuing. "In the tunnel, enchantment was there. There was light; Ava was utterly transfixed."

The Master's eyes brightened.

"Ah, yes! Ava; full of surprises, that one! Fear *yourself* Cass, before you fear her. A fine Knight; a superb strategist. As a warrior – as a woman – she understands the supreme virtue inherent in the unexpected. Never underestimate the power of surprise, Caspian. It can bring down the mightiest force, no matter how corrupt, how black. It can confound the mightiest heart, no matter how pure. Swords have two edges, even here – especially here."

The Mage's look was grave.

"Two edges – then You – what about You?"

"You grow perceptive," the Wizard observed. Now Cass paced before Him, his anger growing as quickly as his suspicions grew to utter certainty.

"*It's a game, isn't it?* It *really* is a game; it has been from the very beginning."

"Not all of it," said the Master.

"Then my power…"

"Yes – it's real. What is happening here, what is happening to *you* – is real. The shreds of reality are actually built into this, all of this. The powers are real, so is the danger. So are the challenges – call them 'tests', if you like."

Cass stared at the man, if it were a man, on the stone.

"A game – and 'tests'; and a 'thing' we call the Queen."

"Tests, yes. And that 'Thing'. You see, the limits of power are part of it, and of the game. Even the 'Queen' is ruled by this, up to a point, of course – an interesting creature, 'entity' I suppose you would say. A *very* evil entity, and One which is as old as time itself."

Cass came to Him.

"Can It be beaten? Can *You* defeat Her – 'It'?"

"'Beaten' – that's not quite the right word, not the best *premise* in this case, I feel certain. You might reconsider that. But, yes, I raised It. I shall put It down when it is time – I believe," said the Master.

The young man before him clenched his fists in anger.

"You *'believe'*?! When it's *'time'*? So the solitaire game in my room…"

"…Brought you onto the board."

"And I can *die* here?" demanded Cass.

"Oh, absolutely – or worse even, you can stay here indefinitely," said the Master calmly, watchfully, for the young man's fury now erupted in a mad rush.

"All of this! *A test.* All of this – you raised that – *that Thing* – You brought me here! *All of this – to 'test' me?* What in Hell does that make You? What kind of man does that make You?"

"What does that make me?" the Wise One pondered. "Oh, at the very least a horrible man, I'll wager, perhaps a very bad man. Yet also a damn fine wizard, and a smart one. More importantly, Caspian Hythe—*what kind of man will it make you?* A good man, a better man, I think – and a damn fine Apprentice."

Cass stared at the Wizard in frank disbelief.

"I am *not* Your Apprentice."

The Master rose from His seat on the stone and stepped behind it as He spoke.

"You are already. You will be yet more of one – when you defeat Her." The Wizard's face and form seemed clad in moonlight as He stepped back, away from Cass.

"Listen, Caspian, listen well. There are three more Elementals – they are not Mine, nor It's. They belong to themselves. Their powers are as ancient, and as potent, as the Thing that rules this space now. They have their own loves and hatred, their own need for vengeance, something you will learn to exploit at need. They have their own dangers – even as It's servants – *what appear as Rabbit, Cat and Hare* – have theirs."

The Mage rushed forward for the Master's voice floated as did His robes, awash in light as pure, as ethereal as the stars above them.

"Wait!" Cass cried.

"You see," said the Master, and His voice seemed more hollow, more distant than ever. "You see how hungry you are, young Mage? For answers, to discover the truth? *What dost Thou desire?* You will make a fine Apprentice – before the end – *you* will ask *Me;* you will do so gladly."

There was almost nothing left of the Master to see, yet, in desperation, the Mage called after Him.

"Wait! If I defeat It, if this place falls – what of the game? *What about Ava? Is Ava real? Or is the Knight part of the game? If I destroy this space – will I lose my Knight?"*

Caspian Hythe ran forward, toward the form suddenly indistinguishable with the trees and the night. Finally, he halted; the Master was truly gone.

The Mage was utterly alone.

His whisper reached only the stars; stars as cold, as pitiless as the wind that carried away his words.

"Wait. Wait. Who are You?"

Shaken to the core, he turned. From the dark before him, growing clearer, and clearer – he saw a door. He went to it, opened it, and stepped through.

He was back in the hallway of the Hatter's house; the Knight stood before him; fear was in her eyes.

Then, unexpectedly and most dreadfully –
many things happened at once.

Chapter 25

JUST/A CELL

The stink of moldering straw, of dank earth and wet stone was overpowering.

As Cass finally regained consciousness, it was the smell that hit him first, not his sense of horror at the bitter taste of betrayal – nor the ache in his jaw and head.

Under all of it; a faint scent, sickly sweet, rank with menace.

It's blood; most of it fresh.

Thy blood and bone feed wood and stone...

He remembered now how it had happened – that he had ended up here; he sighed deeply.

The sigh finished in a bout of coughing. On the floor, on his side, his ribs ached nearly as much as his head. The low rustling sound that came from the straw just paces away made him freeze. Something was crawling there, snuffling at the blood, blood that oozed from its own dark, indistinct form, even as that blood was disappearing into the thirsty dry straw. It came into his head and he immediately did it without question – he blew air as hard as he could toward the thing that moved like no rat he could imagine.

Whatever it was, it settled into the straw and crawled away, into the darkly shadowed end of the cell.

Get up; get off the floor now.

Excellent advice, even if self given; nearly impossible to effect, for when he rolled to his side again, and attempted the simple expedient of 'up', the weight of his shackles pulled him down again. Yet now he was on his knees, at least, and there he stayed while his surroundings grew clearer and infinitely more threatening.

'I hear the Dungeon is rather nice…
You die – but then again so does she…'
Damn Caterpillar – not quite yet.

The light of firebrands flickered on the mossy, stonework walls of the cell that was wide and long and very dark at its furthest reaches. On one wall, piled with orts of old charred wood, and straw, and sad with disuse, the soot- blackened maw of a fireplace could be seen in the gloom. The chain securing his shackles was set into a stone on the floor. With an oaken wine cask set beside it, the door was before him; it was of heavy, dark wood, with iron bars set in the high, narrow window. It bore iron bands and bolts in every place he would have put them himself, had he intended to design a space to confound escape.

A light spear from under the door promised that a hallway or another room lay just outside. The Mage curled himself up, putting his back to the door. His cloak was still on his shoulders, concealing his actions as he searched vainly for his sword, his wand, or his leather bag.

It was the wand that he wanted.

"You won't find it."

The voice was low, triumphant – and female, and it came from the darkest corner of the cell, leaving the speaker veiled in shadow.

"Find what?" asked the Mage, stumbling up finally, onto his feet.

"Oh," continued his watcher. "She made sure it was still on you when she brought you in. So well concealed; it took me some time to find it. The Knight clearly wanted you here. Why she wanted to leave you armed – that is less clear. I can only imagine what Her Majesty's Guards thought, looking down on your Lady – when she appeared at the Palace door with – her trophy?"

There was a sound of movement; his visitor had risen and now moved closer.

"Do you even know who I am? You will know. You will know."

"You are the Duchess," he replied.

She stepped into the light, tall, her face lovely but grim, her blue eyes bright with purpose. She held out her hand – on her palm was his wand. The Duchess moved past him to the door, placing his wand on the wine cask, in full view.

"You will know whom you have injured, whose life it is that you – in your arrogance, with one fell deed – have rendered empty, useless, lonely beyond imagining."

"Your Grace, please, let me speak."

She gave a mirthless laugh.

"Speak? What is there to say? You are alive and awake, before me with every faculty save that of escape. You will have all, at your fingertips – when I kill you."

From her sleeve, she drew a short, stout dagger – light glittered off the finely honed blade.

Ŧ

"This way," he commanded.

The Thane's deep voice echoed in the chamber. The Queen's Ombudsman cast a quick look at the Knight. His conversation with the Thane had been brief and now he left the Thane.

That one again regarded the Knight as she left her position of wait in the light of the Palace's high windows, and approached him.

Unknown to the Thane was the outcome of the long past interview in the drawing room of the slain Duke. Beyond his immediate knowledge were the travails of the Knight and her escort once they had left that place. His Liege had merely told him of Her desire to receive the Mage – and only the Mage – in the Royal presence.

The Thane had taken the appropriate steps. The battle in the dell had been revealing – of the men he had sent, none had returned. That indicated the unexpected scope of the powers of the Mage and his Knight. It did not reveal their relationship; the Thane had drawn his own conclusions.

It was therefore something of a surprise when the young woman now before him had appeared from the copse near the Palace, her sword in one hand, and in the grip of the other, her unconscious escort, whom she dragged to the doors. Now, as the Knight crossed the immense Hall, the Thane appraised her anew.

Fair. Fierce. A fine warrior, one I would add to my ranks, if I could.

Yet now, see how a strange look sits in her eyes – one I had not marked when first we met. She is hardened, tempered she is, like a blade.

Yet, within those eyes there lies barely hidden – the weight of unshed tears. And more – what is this light along her brow – most evident only in the darkest of shadow?

Sword, wand, and sac – the Knight's weapons were intact, at Her Majesty's strict command. The Thane preceded Ava down the Hall, their footfalls soft on the polished marble tiles spreading like a frozen river of black ice. Alert and calm, Ava's gaze rose up as they entered a soaring atrium. High windows, glassed and woven with intricately forged metal marked the upper space. From the floors above, the sound of voices filtered down, echoing from the arched doorways lining the chamber.

Are these the voices of the living – or of the dead?

On the ground floor, within one of the arched doorways, movement caught the sharp eyes of the Knight, and she slowed her steps. Deep within the dark space, shadows seemed to move and flicker, vanishing when her vision fixed on them directly. Nowhere could she see any actual forms that might have cast them, yet move the shadows did.

She commands the Dark.

What of the Light?

And the Mage – which does he command?

"This way, my Knight," came the soft reproof ahead and she fell back into step. At the end of the vast Hall, a high, heavy door loomed. Masked and armed, Door Wardens stood on either side, dressed in the bold and threatening livery of the Black Queen. The Thane stood to one side as the Knight reached the door. He held her eyes with his for a long moment; then he made a slight bow. He turned and left her, vanishing into an alcove nearby.

The Knight regarded the door, with its shining wood, with its designs of silver hearts worked over the lintel and emblazoned on the heavy metal bar on its face. Her gloved hand reached out; she took hold of the bar, gripping it firmly.

Then Ava Fitzalan, Chevalière, thrust the door open and passed within.

Ŧ

"How dare you – how dare you insult me by lying to me?"

The impact of her hand across Cass' face rang in the cell like a thunderclap. He had tried again to speak. The Mage made no attempt to avoid the blow; the force of her hand had driven him backward two steps.

The Duchess' face was pale with rage and the dagger shook in her trembling hand.

"Do you dare to say now that you did not kill the Duke? That you and that cursed Knight, alien to all mercy, to all things moral and sound – did not kill my husband, an innocent, unarmed man, helpless in the night?"

Cass' fingers rose to his lip and came away wet with his own blood. Distraught, desperate for vengeance, the woman stood just paces away; the dagger was raised, her fist knotted tightly about the hilts.

Yet the Mage was silent, immobile. His eyes seemed to burn in the gloom.

One strike; she may have time to strike only once.

Yet – from here, I can reach her.

I can break her neck.

Do I even need to touch her?

To the Duchess, the eyes of the bound man had begun to change, growing darker, brighter, blacker – even as dark as those of the Black Queen, black, limitless, like pools whose bottoms are floored within the pits of Hell. Taller he seemed suddenly, with his shoulders broad, his hands strong, as though the shackles he bore did not exist. A flush crept over the features of the Mage, over his hands. He looked down upon the Duchess. She gasped then stepped back, away from what had seemed to be merely a man bound, helpless, waiting only to die.

"By the gods," she said. "Who are you? What kind of thing can you be?"

The Mage made no answer; words had come to him again and he must needs listen.

What could you not do?
What would you not do?
Yet think, Cass, think.
And forbear.

He exhaled deeply. The gaze he cast upon the Duchess now was one of sadness as he reached to his pocket to withdraw something small, something that he carefully held out to the Lady, on his palm. His words were low but plaintive.

In token, in love,
As the ring on your own.
Hand to hand,
Heart to heart,
Shall our promise be known.

The Duchess cried out; there in the hand of the Mage was the Duke's ring. The dagger slipped from her fingers, landing on the straw at their feet and with tears on her face, the Duchess took the ring of her husband from the hand of the man before her.

"He did not fail. He bade me tell you – of his love, Lady."

"He said that?"

"He did; before we freed him from Her bondage, myself and my Knight."

"Where is my Lord?" the Duchess asked sadly.

"Light surrounds him – more I cannot say," the Mage replied. He knelt and retrieved the dagger, then held it out to the Lady. For a long moment, she stared at it, then at him. She wiped her tears and taking the knife from him, she replaced it in its sheath in her boot. Returning to the wine cask, she retrieved the wand, surprised to find how warm it felt in her hand. From her gown pocket, she took out his leather bag; then turned to present his weapons to the Mage.

He stood waiting in silence, his hands at his sides.

His open shackles lay in the straw at his feet.

Chapter 26

SALAMANDER

The Mage went to the door, listening. He turned to the Duchess.

"Who knows that you are here?"

"None but the Guard I bribed."

"Lady – it would have cost your life had the Queen known."

"Nay, she hates you Mage."

He made a grim laugh. "Like the fire hates the log. Where is my Knight?"

She gave him a grave look.

"She is gone to Her Majesty – now, I believe."

"To the Queen? God. Then once again – we have run out of time. I need… I need… there!"

He ran to the fireplace in the wall.

"Stay back – do not speak!" he said to the Duchess.

Cass stood before the fireplace; he became still and stillness, portentous and terrible filled the cell. One by one, the brands on the walls burned with violence – then each died away, to extinguish completely. Once again, there came the unfathomable look into the Sorcerer's eyes, as he surrendered to what he saw, what he felt, to the mystery within him, to the invocation that slowly came to his lips. As if in dream, but with surety, with grave purpose, his hand went to the leather sac once more on his belt – and he drew forth the card.

His voice resounded in the prison like distant drums, one voice among many, and in horror, the Duchess backed away, until she stood hard against the locked door while before her transformed a man into a being she had never seen before.

I call the South…
I call the South… of Wands, the King.
Phoenix ash and poison's sting.
Rise! Bring Fire's flaming breath,
The SALAMANDER'S power – Death!
Woe to all I see at hand!
With scepter's power, I Command
The lion's vengeance, fierce and dark!
I call Thee – SALAMANDER – Hark!
I call the South….

The card flew from his hand, igniting and burning into cinders whose ashes flew forward, joining the soot and straw and charred wood in the fireplace, and the entire mass burst into flames, falling in upon itself, imploding – and a deeply echoing, hollow bellow erupted in the cell, deafening the woman at the door.

From far within the fireplace's maw – a hole within a hole appeared, growing, roaring, and hissing as icy water and fire met and mated, and blazing flames surged into the room. Fire ignited the straw at the Mage's feet, flames spread to the sides and rear of the cell, fire hungrily reached toward the Duchess, blue fire arced like lightning, encircling the Mage entirely – yet he neither moved nor burned.

The Duchess cried out; she did not speak but in her mind were flames, flames and the terrible image of her own death and that of the Mage.

As from the heart of the fire surging forth from the grate, a creature formed. It rose, higher and higher until it stood nearly man high, and it faced the Sorcerer. Where the fire met and conquered the coldest and blackest depths of the Salamander's realm, a thing that was not a lizard, not a

Salamander, but a being clothed in flame and water
raised itself before the Mage. Fire came from its wide
nostrils; living flames curled along the long mane
that fluttered, bright with cinders, behind its noble
brow, and powerful shoulders; the being spoke and
the Duchess fell to her knees.

> *The South replies....*
> *Feel my force, the water's bane.*
> *The Lion's flashing eyes, his mane*
> *Are all my Faces. Life expires*
> *In these, my Elemental fires.*
> *Wilt Thou burn? I offer Thee*
> *The Turnéd Card – Thy path made free!*
> *But Death awaits in places green.*
> *Her savage heart – Her vengeance keen!*
> *She falls to rise. Thy passage paved*
> *By Loss – the Life by Water saved.*

A torrent of wind rushed from the fireplace – and
with nothing less than a thunderclap, the door of the
cell burst open, tearing off its hinges. The
Salamander lowered, disappearing into its own
flames, back down into the dark hole spinning

within the grate. The fire dwindled down and down, finally settling into cold ash; there was nothing more to see in the fireplace.

The cell, however, was on fire. Fire was spreading out the door into the hallway of the dungeon itself. The Mage swept the Duchess into his arms and bolted through the open door into a corridor paved with dark stone, its cold walls hung with lit sconces. Fire still found its way after them, sending brilliant licks of heat along the walls, and the Mage set the Duchess down to the cries of 'Fire' ringing through the dungeon, rising with the sound of warning bells, that, all too soon, would be answered by the Queen's men.

The Lady knew her way; with the Mage just behind her, the two raced down the corridor.

"This way," she cried and the Mage took the lead, as they turned abruptly to reach the upper level – and the way out.

The Mage stopped dead in his tracks – his arm was out, barring the passage of the Duchess, and very nearly her sight of the thing that waited in the passageway ahead.

"It took you long enough, Mage! But you do not disappoint!"

The tones were liquid but vicious, alive with the same malice Cass had seen in the pine glade, and the Cat's tail lashed excitedly. The beast stood right before them, a wickedly triumphant grin across its face; the Duchess paled when she saw the infernal thing and heard the Mage's harsh whisper.

"That is what took the Duke, Lady."

"Here you are at last, and with the Duchess, whose husband died so well," the Cat purred. It took a step forward – and its size changed. Now it stood as tall as a mastiff; its growl echoed in the corridor.

"But you, dear Mage, you have my thanks – for now I can kill you both – at the same time."

ℱ

"Whatever is wrong, Mage? No greeting? Alas! No matter – Cat got your tongue, regardless!"

The Cat sprang forward. Without hesitation, the Mage reached to the strut of the sconce on the wall, tearing it from its perch. With a crash, it landed in front of the beast.

"Oh, such fun!" it cried. "Thy game pleases me well – how does it please thee? Is it too soon to say?'

The Cat padded around the obstacle toward the Mage and the Duchess, its form growing larger as it moved, when, without warning, from the adjoining corridor – a squad of the Queen's Guards ran forward, nearly colliding with the thing before them. The Cat turned and its claws gutted the first man within reach, his scream fading as he dropped. The Cat took him in its jaws; shaking him as a terrier might a rat, it flung the streaming carcass into the mass of men, running in panic in all directions. The dead man's blood had no time to pool on the floor – both straw and stone greedily absorbed it.

The Cat quickly cornered another victim against the wall, and sank its now inch-long teeth into his back – as Cass pulled the Duchess away.

"Go – go now," he said; the Lady pulled up her skirts and vanished down the hall as the Cat, tired of its sport with the crushed body of the downed Guard, turned again to the Sorcerer.

"Bad Mage! I had so wanted to re-unite the Duchess with her Duke!" it said mournfully.

The Mage backed away from the beast, drawing the bloodthirsty thing after him.

"It's me you want after all, isn't it? But you should consider carefully – your Lady may yet want me alive."

"Oh, my Sorcerer; there are so many degrees of 'alive' – let us play again now, let us play a game of fight and flight, of flesh – and blood – all yours, and all without hope."

Cass took to his heels, his race down the hall and quick turn left him in a blind alley – he whirled about to see the Cat blocking any chance of escape. It leaped – but as it did so, the hand of the Mage rose and the air coalesced before the airborne creature. With a savage howl, the Cat collided with the rippling, invisible, but solid wall of air, sliding downward. In a flash, it had set its talons into the air and clawed its way over the top, just as the Mage ran past, the air collapsing into its normal state around him. Laughing horribly, the beast raked its claws at the Mage as he swept past; they sheared open his shirt, leaving bleeding welts across the man's bared chest.

Backing away, in desperation, Cass pulled open the bag at his belt – his hand came out, a piece of mushroom on his palm – and he threw it with all his might at the now enormous animal stalking forward. The Cat rose, caught the piece in mid-air and bolted it down. It purred mightily, and to Cass' horror – it grew even more massive.

"Is there any more?" it asked. "A tasty treat – and see how well it suits me, Mage!"

Snarling, the thing sprang forward again –but its size had slowed it – and the Sorcerer had also leaped, up the wall. Catching hold of the strut of a sconce, Cass pulled himself up, his hand reaching for the railing of the stairs above. He struggled to lift himself – and the bag at his belt pulled free.

Cass swung from his perch, watching as his bag fell. It landed at the feet of the Cat – who avidly devoured the bag, in turn looking up greedily – as the strut that held the Mage above its head – creaked loudly, loosened – and pulled free from the wall.

In a stifling stream of stones and dust, the Mage fell. He landed hard, all the air knocked out of him, onto the floor. The Cat was waiting; it caught him as he rose to his feet; with one mighty swing of its huge paw, it sent the Mage crashing headfirst into the wall opposite.

Torn, bleeding, bruised, Caspian Hythe roused to find himself on the floor on his back – with the Cat looming over him.

Hot saliva dripped down from a gape wide enough to swallow a dog. With slow precision and infinite pleasure, the infernal beast carefully set its teeth into the Mage's shoulder; the doomed man cried out; his own blood now dripped down upon him from the creature's mouth as it withdrew its teeth – and purred deafeningly.

"Bit by bit, piece by piece – so grows my appetite and the certainty of your fate, Mage. Is it not a game fit for a Queen? I think we have had enough of appetizers. Come, Sorcerer, let us see how close we can bring you – to death – and back again."

It opened its mouth wide. The beast drew close; the Cat's hot breath was on his face.

Suddenly the animal halted.

The Cat's eyes widened horribly and a choking sound came from its great mouth and throat. It pulled back onto its haunches and now dark blood – not the blood of the man beneath it –

began to drip from the animal's mouth. The creature staggered away from the Mage – great heaving coughs came from the thing and it circled, stumbling – as slowly but surely – the Cat's form began to shrink.

Smaller and smaller; one last dreadful roar choked off into a strangled scream arose from the Cat. Moment by moment, the body of the animal shifted, ever slighter in size until the sound of crushing bone and streaming fluid reverberated in the dungeon.

Before the Mage's eyes, the monster fell in upon itself. Its fur and flesh scattered in puffs along the floor, puffs that also shrank ever smaller. A low dreadful, unimaginable sound came from the masses of dwindling bone and blood and fur – with a soft whirring – the entire creature vanished from sight.

Even the blood on the floor, steaming and foaming was soon gone – it its place, a pale blue light shone – and with a savage arc of brilliance, there, in place of the Black Queen's monstrous servant – was the Mage's leather sac.

With a groan, the Sorcerer hauled himself upright. He barely kept his footing, he still bled freely – but he was alive. He staggered forward and retrieved the bag – as he raised it, something small, bright and shining fell from it, to land at his feet.

It was the golden key from the table in the corridor of tears.

Ava.

He put it into his pocket, returning the bag to its place at his belt.

"So much for mushrooms."

Cass walked to the nearest door in the hall. He stood before it, his eyes closed in deep concentration.

With a soft click, the door swung open to admit him and he passed through.

Chapter 27

SAVING THROW

It took several moments for the Knight's eyes to adjust to the dark just inside the heavy door of the Ebony Hall.

In her mind, the voice came – female, cool, with a low guttural undertone that was not unfamiliar to Ava.

Ava. Welcome – my Knight – advance.

I have been waiting for you. I saw it all, you know.

I was there, in the Hatter's house as the Mage came back through the door.

How will he ever forgive you?

I saw it all.

At Her words, the desolate Hall of the Black Queen vanished from Ava's sight and, once more, the Knight stood in the hallway of the Hatter's house.

The door had opened and Cass had appeared; his face was grim, his eyes wild. As the door had shut behind him, his hand came out, gripping the Knight's shoulder. He had steadied himself, then half stumbled to lean against the wall across from the fateful door.

"I should never have brought you here," he said.

The Knight joined him as he grew increasingly distraught.

"What? What do you mean – 'brought me' here?"

"I should never have stepped onto the board! Don't you understand? You – me – it's real, but it isn't. Are you real, Ava?"

"Of course I am. Cass, what happened in there?"

Ava turned and took a step toward the closed door – the Mage threw himself in front of her, blocking her way.

"No! Don't touch it! Don't go in there!"

"Is She in there, Cass?"

He paced away from her in despair, and he shouted, his voice ringing in the hallway.

"The Game is over! I won't play anymore –
do You hear me? I won't play! We are leaving!"

He stared wildly about him and Ava watched
him with mounting fear.

*"Who are you talking to? Is She in there,
Cass?"*

"No! We've got to leave, we must leave now!
Come on."

He dragged her after him, toward the stairs –
she pulled back with all her strength; the Mage's
voice was changing, lowering in the furious
desperation of fear.

*"You will do as I say! You will come with me
now! Must I Command you?"*

They stood face to face in the hall, frozen, he
with his shaking hands gripping her shoulders, she,
pulling back, away from him, aghast.

"Those are the words of tyrants, my Lord,"
she said.

Aghast – he released her and stepped away,
his eyes first on the door, then on her.

"My Knight, I can no longer control it – I no
longer want to," he gasped. "I've got to get out of
here – while I can – while I still can."

The Knight looked on him; unutterable
sadness and pity was in her eyes.

"You will, my Lord. You will."

Her gloved fist went hard into his face.

The Mage fell in a senseless heap at her feet.
The Knight reached down; taking hold of his cloak,
she dragged Cass back to the closed door.

To the door of the very room he had entered
and from which he had returned, from whose wood,
from whose space beyond – rang the sound of claws
savagely drawn across the door's surface.

Claws... claws at your throat.

As before – with a click, the door had swung
slowly inward. Dragging the Mage after her, the
Knight had stepped across the threshold.

☦

Now, the Knight drew a deep breath; again, she
stood in the present – she stood in the Queen's
Ebony Hall.

A fireplace deep and long loomed along one
side; a man might have stood upright within it.
Flames licked upward from the grate piled high with

logs. But no warmth came forth, even as cinders rose like scintillating stars up the giant flue.

The Knight stepped forward. As she did, shadows crept in to greet her, slowly feeling their way from along the walls, crawling across the brilliant black floor. With them came the muffled echoes of voices – the broken tones of unrequited sorrow, the muttered curses of implacable, pining vengeance, and unabated – the low cries of eternal torment.

"My dear Chevalière. Welcome."

The voice was real; it came from the woman seated on the throne set like a bastion in the centre of this sanctum – the sanctum of the Black Queen.

Forward the Knight strode, her steps muted on the mirror-like surface at her feet. Ava looked down on a floor that became more and more transparent. The space below the floor was slowly filling with mist. From those frigid, ever- shifting depths, hands were rising, reaching upward, and the pale, drawn faces of those below turned up, their glowing eyes seeking those of their Dark Liege.

This was the heart of the domain; the throne of the Lady reflected it. It was tall and deeply carved;

its layers of rich furs that did nothing to belie the essence of its foundations – it remained cold, hard, and uncompromising.

The Knight halted some paces before the seat. Calmly, she apprised the woman who sat, regal, poised, her rule inviolate. Calmly the Queen apprised her guest. However, the Lady's eyes brightened suddenly – as the floor close beside the Knight's boot buckled and rippled – and a clawed hand rose. Seeming to feel its way more by scent than by touch, it crossed the boundary between the Dark and the world Above – and seized the Knight by her ankle.

It was a grip as hard and cruel, as searing as ice – like poison, a wave of pain spread upward through the Knight's leg. Her head swam with the scent of blood, of blood and corruption rising upward and a low growl echoed in the cavernous Hall. In answer, from all points of the chamber, the voices of those imprisoned here rose to a discordant chorus, a hateful hiss of tainted waves breaking upon a cursed shore.

The talons squeezed, wrapped tightly about the young woman's leg – and pulled downward. For a dizzyingly painful moment, Ava's boot was below the floor.

Her jaw set; in a flash, her sword was in her hand – without a downward glance, the Knight made a lightning fast strike toward her own foot. In one sweep, the blade severed the hand at the grey wrist. A piercing howl of something that had never been animal faded away and the wrist withdrew below the floor. The severed hand, twisting in agony, folded in upon itself, disintegrating into dark, shifting ash. The flames in the fireplace surged and Ava felt a cold blast of wind reach her from the grate, a wind that carried the ashes away, across the shining floor.

The Queen smiled.

The voices ceased their grim cacophony, growing more and more indistinct – and the Knight stood before the Queen with a naked blade in her hand, from whose edge dark blood steamed.

Brazen and cold, the Black Queen's laughter filled the somber Hall.

"Well done, my Knight! But before you strike again – let me offer you refreshment."

From behind the wide, high seat were the sounds of movement.

Carrying a silver chalice set upon a silver tray, the Queen's Cupbearer came from behind the throne and advanced, halting before the Knight. Ava slowly sheathed her sword; slowly, she knelt down upon one knee. The Chevalière gazed upon the one before her – at the wide, dark eyes, the white face with its cropped ebony locks. Frozen tears lay on the cheeks of the Cupbearer, the child whose spirit had written in her own blood on a man's tomb, a child bound in torment even as he was bound – the spirit of Alice Liddell.

The Queen smiled at the spirit that held the server.

"Is she not pretty, my Cupbearer? This is almost as merry a party as that at the Hatter's fine table. We should have him here, too – call him, my lovely little one – and you, Knight – shall I make it so that you can hear her call? Her voice is dulcet and sweet to the ear."

Wide and open grew the child's mouth, like a cankered rosebud, for from the depths of her throat nothing came save for the low, terrible voices of the shadows that flirted at the edge of vision round the chamber.

"Oh, wait – I do apologise. Let me make it – so that you may *understand* her."

It was a growl at first, guttural, biting as might be the snarl of an animal – and then came a soft whisper, as words took form out of the child's senseless moan.

"Soul and sorrow – set us free."

At this, an appalling sound came from across the vast chamber – a door there flew open with a crash. Through it came two figures.

First, the Rabbit strode forward. With its red eyes shining, it walked triumphantly in on its hind legs, and its nails clicked on the floor's slick surface. It turned suddenly; in its high, reedy voice, it called back, into the restless shadows crowding the space beyond the door.

"Hurry it up! We don't want to keep them waiting, do we?"

The sound of metal upon metal, of sighs, of chains dragging along the floor – through the doorway, on his hands and knees, the Hatter crawled. Blood smeared the shackles that bound him

331

wrist and ankle; a sheen of blood was in his wake as he crawled toward the throne – it was a stain that quickly vanished into the black tiles.

The child that had been Alice watched the Hatter's painful progress – powerless she was, unable to move from the Queen's chair, unable to go to him. A low, strangled sob came from the child's throat and the Knight looked on the Queen with anger, with impotent hatred – and despair. For now, it seemed that even with all her strength, all her speed, and all her skill, she could not win. Nothing could thwart the Thing that sat upon the throne, and all she had risked seemed utterly lost, her stratagem without hope.

How can I release them?

If Cass were here – could even the Mage, with his powers – how could even he prevail?

Does he yet live?

Help us – help him. Help me.

It came – for a second, the horrific chorus of hellish voices ceased – calm descended on the Knight. She was able to breathe again, as if she had suddenly regained the surface of a stagnant, clutching pool of dark water – light came into her mind, and she heard once more.

> *From the dark, within that place,*
> *Where soul and sorrow share one tortured face,*
> *Draw hope; take strength from where it hides.*
> *In courage – see how liberty abides.*
> *Call Thou ….the North.*

Jarring the Knight – shouts, and laughter came from the dark beyond the door – in a tumbled heap, with her hair and robes in disarray, the Duchess fell forward onto her knees through the doorway. A Guard appeared behind her. He laughed again; his boot came back, ready to strike the Lady who glared up at him, her eyes proud, bold – in defiance.

The man's leg was savagely kicked out from under him. He landed heavily on the floor inside the chamber. There he lay. In shock and fear, he looked up at the Thane who had leapt to the Duchess' side, and now stood, with drawn sword, glowering over the Guard. The Guard crawled back beyond the door as the Thane sheathed his blade, knelt at the Duchess' side, and carefully raised her from the floor. Haughty and calm, the Lady preceded him into the Hall. Beside the fireplace that gave no warmth, they stood, silent, waiting. The Black Queen looked about her.

"Well met, my Duchess! Are we all here? But no – wait! Yes, if my eyes tell me true – we are yet missing – One more! I wonder – who can it be?"

Chapter 28

INITIATIVE

"Faster, Hatter! Can you not see Thy Lady is waiting?"

The Rabbit's harsh voice rang out again and Ava's hand tensed on her sword as the creature savagely struck the crawling man with its walking stick.

The beast drew its arm back, ready to strike again – but a startled gasp came from the animal's throat. Its eyes blazed red and the walking stick slid from its paw, to land clattering on the floor.

The Queen slowly rose from Her chair – the Rabbit came to Her and whispered hoarsely.

"He is fallen, Lady. Cat has fallen Below."

The monarch strode to the Hatter; with Her foot, She shoved him onto the floor, where he struggled with his bonds, struggled to rise even to his knees.

"This is your friend's work," She said in a low voice. "It will cost you dear – shall we see how dear?"

The chained man glared up at Her.

"What can you do to me that you have not done already? I gave Thee life and substance – to my sorrow. The Cat will be but the first to fall; he will not be the last."

Her hand came back to strike him; it was withdrawn and the Dark Lady's face took on a strange look.

"You, Hatter – You shall fall when I do. Will it be soon? I think it shall be never. There will be time for you and I to play again – see how well I play."

She turned on Her heel and paced to the Knight, whom She regarded with a gentle smile.

"How foolish of me," She said. "How foolish, not to see in your strength a power I have never encountered. Your counsel and wisdom are as gifts, unlooked for, but full in blessing and bounty – for what is a reign without wisdom, without conscience? What is life – without new blood? Think what is here – all there is to see – to learn – it is a wondrous place. Here are marvels to delight the senses, to challenge the mind. Here is beauty, whose magical essence would be yours, yours to explore, to

taste, to experience. Stay with me, Chevalière –
teach me to forebear, let me learn the patience and
care that guide your actions. Stay with me – join
your strength to mine, stand with me as an equal.
Take your place beside me – as a beloved sister."

The Knight's thoughts were dark as she heard
these words. It was a game after all – she had played
and it had gained her time and access to the Queen –
for the Knight had been certain of that monarch's
insatiable hunger for the novel, the unexpected. Yet
the Mage had been the lure – and now the Knight
was just as certain that her own danger surpassed his
– and that she might have thrown, only to lose all.

Her fear was mirrored in the face of the man
on the floor.

The Hatter watched in horror, for, as the
Knight had listened to the Queen, as Her words
turned ever gentler, sweeter and more persuasive –
the raiment of the Chevalière had begun a shocking
change.

As dark as ink, shadows had begun to creep –
upward from the black floor – over the boots and
leggings of the warrior. Soothing and persuasive, a
hushed chorus of voices added their tones to the

melodious ones of their Liege. Now the Knight's boots were black, their leather as finely polished as the floor, now her leggings had begun to change, growing darker and richer with each of the Queen's honeyed words – the man in irons could no longer contain himself.

"Stop! Stop now; do not attend Her! Do not listen!"

Stark silence fell in the chamber – with his tongue cleaving to the roof of his mouth, the Hatter fell dumb – and the Knight roused as from the edge of dream. She regarded the Queen with renewed hatred as the warrior's clothing regained its true colours – and Ava strode forward, facing the monarch.

"You lie. What can You give? Little more than bondage, only a mirror's surface – in return, I am to give You a hostage ready to Your hand – for how would the Mage dare to strike – with me at Your side? It is he that You seek – that You desire. I will not procure him for You – not even for my life. I will die unfettered. I will perish untainted by the empty promises that tyranny offers to the desperate."

Savage fury marked the face of the Dark Lady. She stepped forward, Her arm drawn back to strike, the fingers suddenly long and clawed – when the great doors flew open with a crash.

Into the Hall strode the Queen's Guards; the two tallest, at their head, dragged forward a man. With torn clothing, bloody, but his head high, they held in close captivity between them the Mage.

"Ah," breathed the Queen. "Behold – the conqueror. Look at him, Hatter. Will he be the one to ease your pain, to buy you one more day of miserable existence? Not by strength – but by submission, perhaps? He knows – that if he stays I will bring an end to your suffering."

The Hatter stiffened proudly on his knees.

"Only death can do that, Lady.

"There is nothing beyond that veil, Hatter."

"There is peace," he said.

"Are you certain? 'Peace and eternal rest'? *Were it so – however did I manage to bring you here?* It is a paradox, I believe! Nothing can change that!"

At that word – the Mage's mind began to race.

339

Paradox – premise.

Change the premise – what is the premise – the premise is – that She can do – what?

"Release the Mage," the Queen cried. "He has no real power here. In the heart of my realm, my rule is absolute. Therefore, my power is absolute. He knows how the game must end."

A light shone from the eyes of the man in chains; it was Ava who responded.

"Endings have a way of changing, even as stories do."

The Queen came to her.

"You had your moment. It has passed. The Mage is wiser than you; poor, foolish soldier. Can you not see that it is he, who will stand beside me? Your consort has outgrown you, child. He is ready now for one worthier. For one who can teach him what he desires to know – and, oh, he desires greatly. Is that not so, Sorcerer? Of course it is! If you come to me, you will see how well it will suit you – you will see how I will free both Hatter and child – and, also the Knight. Yes – all may go free."

Without a glance at the Knight, Cass strode across the Hall and stood before the Queen. He was silent for many moments.

"What You offer – I already have. What You would pay me – You would pay in coin I cannot use. Do You see?"

"What I see – is that you no longer fear the Dark. That is unwise – a little fear is a good thing. I can promise you – before the end, *you will come to me. You will ask me – you will do so gladly.*"

The Mage stood stunned as one struck by lightning.

"So, command me," the Queen continued. "Command me as you did her. What will you command, my Mage? That I die – I cannot die, not in this world, nor in any. That I fall? I fall only to rise, my Sorcerer. *What wouldst Thou command – what couldst Thou not command me to do?*"

He turned from Her, blinded by those words in Her mouth, by horror and the anguish of almost certain defeat – the ready shadows of the Lady's realm were coursing forward again, eager to fasten on them, to claim the Knight, the Hatter – and himself. Yet as he stood, bereft of hope, amidst the chorus of the damned, he heard the Knight. He turned to her – her lips had not moved; she stood silent and grave. Yet he heard her, her words deep and harsh, as clearly, as though her lips were at his ear.

> *The limits of power are part of the game.*
> *She rules here.*
> *Change the premise.*
> *You do not have to vanquish Her to win.*
> *Do not command that She be vanquished.*

The Mage exhaled; his head bowed for an instant – then he turned back to the Queen.

"Thou hast asked me – therefore, I shall Command Thee, Lady. *I Command Thee –* **Thou dost not rule.**"

The Queen's face went white – and a great shuddering lament came from deep inside the throne at Her back. Cracks, hair-line, but deep, appeared. They rose, spreading, penetrating the foundation of the Dark One's seat as frost cuts it way across a window pane. Dark blood seeped from the throne and the Queen cried out – the devastation swept from throne to floor; fractures fine and deep tore across the once perfect marble surface of the Ebony Hall.

She turned back to the Mage. Her face was livid with rage, Her teeth – sharp and white – clenched into a snarl. She raised both Her hands, both clawed, and reached toward the Sorcerer, who did not blench.

"I call …the South," he said.

A faint sound, as of the bellowing of distant dragons – it came from deep within the massive fireplace, and the bellows pealed louder and louder. The stones about the fireplace shook, and shivered, and began to fall and a tempest of wind erupted from far within the grate – a gale that was no longer frigid with ancient death but hot, blazing with new life and brilliant light – and fire.

From out of the heart of that fire, whose flames licked ravenously up the flue – a form emerged. Like a lizard but utterly unlike, it rolled from the grate to rise upright in the room, first on four legs – then on two, and flame – white hot and blue, seethed forth from the cauldron in the grate, where water and fire met, and mated.

The Duchess pulled free from the Thane; he joined his men scattering from the deadly rain of fire, racing for the doors, in horror of the thing that had come from fire, and brought fire to life.

The South…replies.

It was a voice like the voice of storm; the walls of the Hall buckled and tore as the Salamander rose in flames, its mane igniting, its eyes as bright and as glowing as the dragon's – its form shifting between man and beast, immortal bird and reptile.

The floor crumpled and an enormous crevasse ripped across the very centre of the Hall. Piece by piece, the walls themselves began to fall – the Black Queen stood on the edge of the abyss, and screamed in impotent rage – it was a scream cut short – She turned – to see the Duchess behind Her – that Lady's dagger was lodged deep in the back of her Liege. With a shriek that split the ceiling, the Dark Queen stumbled and fell back – Her form vanished below the lip of the chasm.

From the cavern, a spume of white hot fire rose up – a dreadful scream came from the Rabbit and its form began to change, as, layer by layer, its aspect stripped away, until only the shadow of something dark, bestial – its red eyes shining – was left. It lasted only an instant, obscured in a rain of fire and ash.

The Queen was gone. In the midst of the firestorm, her creator sat upon the floor, his chains burst and in pieces about him. An unearthly blue light suffused his features – with smiling face and tears on his cheeks, he opened both arms wide, admitting the spirit of the child he had loved. Clasping one another closely, they were lost to view. Light, seething and blue curled about them; the two forms became one and then indistinguishable.

The Salamander towered in the Hall. Its mighty head shook from side to side as, with a roar, it lay waste to what roof remained.

The Mage looked beside him – the Knight stood there. He took her by the arm and they ran; their flight ended before the fireplace, from whose maw uncanny blue flames surged and roiled.

The Sorcerer stepped into the light; he held out his hand to her.

She hesitated only a moment, then reached for him.

Taking her hand in a grasp of steel – the Mage drew her after him, into the flames, and the Knight knew no more.

Chapter 29

CRUNCH

It was a heaving, painful gasp – but her lungs still served her.

Head spinning, with her body stinging yet numb, the Knight sat on the floor. On the old, worn carpet before her – the Mage knelt; she now felt he had both her hands in his, gripping them hard.

"Fitz," he repeated.

"I'm here. Where is here?"

He laughed.

"We're back in the Hatter's parlour."

It was true; they stood to face the same fireplace from which the Salamander had first appeared – an age ago – when the Knight had decided to pursue a little stratagem that had nearly cost them all.

Ava's fingers touched the spot on his face where her fist had struck him.

"I owe you one," he said.

A murmur that grew to a terrifying rumble; the walls of the house had begun to creak.

Now they rocked and with the sound of splintering wood and stone, a rift creased its way across the ceiling, sending down planks and plaster almost on their heads. They gained the door as the walls shuddered and with a long, grating sigh – the entire structure began to collapse. By the time they reached the meadow outside, all that could be seen was a blasted shell, still twisting, groaning in torment.

The sun was setting. Its light gilded the torn and shifting remains of the creator's abode. With a blood red sky behind them, the Mage and the Knight stood etched in gold and watched the house fall in upon itself. High overhead, building in strength, and set afire by the same sun – the clouds of a great storm had begun to gather.

They ran; they ran back along the way they had come.

Now, the Mage took the lead, driving them forward with his pace, racing along the path, one whose vines and thickets no longer clutched at their clothing nor seized their weapons. He was far ahead of Ava as she made her way after him, into what had been the Queen's garden – and stumbled to a halt.

He was gone.

"Cass?"

She drew her sword, whirled around, scanning the way she had come – there was no sign of the Sorcerer either ahead or behind.

"Cass!" Now it was a shout of desperation – and she looked up.

There, out of reach, nearly five meters over the Knight's head – hung the Mage. His body was tightly wrapped, immobile, in the vines of a Nightshade that had found its way up a tree, weaving its snares at eye level. Bound, unconscious – his form swung in the wind.

The Knight sprang forward – with her sword, she hacked at the base of the vine where it joined the ground. An angry hiss came from the plant as layer after layer of bark came away, her blade cutting through the thick chords of green anchoring the plant to its roots. Finally, with a savage low shriek, the vine snapped – the strangling tendrils that bound the Mage gave way – and he landed at her feet.

Ava dragged him away from the tree and its deadly creeper, and dropped over him.

There was no pulse.

He was not breathing.

Ava cried out – her closed fist slammed down on his chest – nothing. She leapt up, her hand stinging – below lay Cass, still, pale – lifeless.

"No. No. I cannot leave you. I will not leave you … here."

Helpless, hopeless – she tore off her gloves, her cloak, and went down upon her knees – a thin line of blood lay in the crease of her palm, where the weight of her sword had rubbed the skin raw. In a daze of despair, she looked at the skin, at the blood and the red, torn flesh beneath it.

"The skin – the skin is all gone. What shall I do now?"

The Knight gasped – and cried out in wonder – she rose to her feet and came to stand directly over the man's body.

"Now – I choose! I choose now my second skin! I choose… the High Priestess."

From nowhere, from everywhere – blue light surged and roiled, enveloping the Knight in a vortex of arcing sapphire. The girl's head swam – then her vision cleared. She looked down upon herself – at her gown and robes of diaphanous silk, her veil of silver, as bright as starlight. Over her chest, she felt the massive solar cross and felt across her brow the weight of the crown, surmounted by lightning, with its full moon matched on either side by lunar discs.

Ava's senses reeled – waves of sensation coursed through her, threatening to bring her to her knees once again. Her hand rose to her cheek; she brushed away the tears there, and spoke – and for the space of a heartbeat, all the lands Under halted and harkened, halted in the midst of demise, of certain fall. Thunder sounded over the garden and the skies were broken with light and shadow – for the High Priestess spoke.

> *I call … the North.*
> *I call the North …*
> *Of Swords – the Knight.*
> *His heart is true, his courage bright.*
> *From the forest, SYLPH appear!*
> *Lord of wind, and flowing air,*
> *From the clouds, command His power—*
> *Come! In this, my desperate hour!*
> *I call …the North!*

Lightning answered overhead, as from all points, clouds, fomenting with blinding light and darkest shadow, raced forth and a blast of wind surged toward the Priestess.

From the living clouds, a form appeared, its long streaming hair crowned with light, its outstretched arms foaming with the might of storm and endless, moving airs. Sky blue and grey, its eyes sought hers in a gaze bright, imperious, grave, and terrible. The Sylph lowered. Its form, like to that of a man bound and bred by shimmering rain, drew near and the Priestess trembled in awe at His approach as, with a voice as soft, as purring as wind and life-giving mists – He spoke.

The North replies!
From the trees, the greenwood home,
Swift as wind, the SYLPH has come!
I rule the tempest. From the North,
The torrents rise, as I come forth.
Beware! The final hours near,
Her heart is black, Her strength is fear!
Her weakness flows – now black and red,

Those tears released – Her secret dread!
If the victory stands undone – turn the Key
And see it won!

The Sylph reached out for the young woman whose robes were already changing back, dissolving. Leather and linen slowly grew back across the Knight. It was the Knight's face that the Sylph gently took in His hands; the Knight's lips He parted, covering them with His own as, with a great sigh – He breathed into the girl in His arms.

Ava staggered back even as the Elemental's body misted over with silver chased cloud and mist and a funnel of wind surrounded Him. The wind passed – He was gone, and Ava Fitzalan fell beside the body of the Mage, pressing her open mouth to his, forcing her lips against those so cold and pale – and she breathed the gift of the Sylph into the lifeless body of the Sorcerer.

Spent, cold, and numb with grief, the Knight drew back upon her knees – as light suffused the Mage's features, spreading across his form – and a breeze as soft as that in spring, carrying the scent of the year's first flowers rose around him.

A great shudder coursed through Cass' frame. He coughed; colour returned. It surged across his face, his chest, and hands. The Knight watched – unable to speak, with her heart torn, watching the Mage come alive – and empty beyond imagining she was, for she was bereft of the power that had consumed her, the glory that had surged through her. Tears wet the girl's cheeks as the Mage rolled to his side – and rose onto his feet, facing her.

She was still some paces from him; she rose too. The smile on his face suddenly melted into horror.

"Watch out!"

A look of shock overspread the Knight's features. Gasping, she turned, agonized – to face the Black Queen just behind her – whose dagger was set deep in the girl's ribs.

Ava slipped to the ground at the Queen's feet, feet shod in fine black boots. Clad now in leather, black and red, and tight across her form, the Queen pulled her dagger from the body of the Knight – She kissed the blade – blood marked the Lady's lips – and She sheathed the dagger once more in Her boot.

At Her feet lay the Knight, blood slowly pooling around her. Cass pulled off his cloak and massed it, then knelt by her side, pressing against the wound. The girl winced but she gazed up at him.

"It's been quite the little adventure – underground," she said.

"It's not over yet – no, don't speak!"

She shook her head.

"Yes. I am glad you came, Cass." Her voice weakened and he brought his head to hers, his lips close to her ear, whispering. The girl's eyes grew wide – then the lids fluttered and closed. The Mage lowered her tenderly to the ground and rose to face the Queen.

"Now my Mage; perhaps we can finally deal in coin that you can use. Look at her – she is dying. She will die. *There is nothing you can do* – not yet do you have the power, not yet do you have the hate, the need for vengeance – to work any incantation that will call her back. *Yet I do – I can – I will.* Stay – and I spare her life. Stay willingly and I send her back – Above – all Thou must do – is ask."

The Sorcerer looked down upon the one still and white at his feet. Ava's lips moved, wordlessly –

around him, the ground trembled; the torrents of the falls were now a trickle, dammed by rubble and stone. Stone fell from the heights, and the pool below churned and raged with ruin. The Mage drew his wand – it lay inert across his palm – it was powerless against the Thing before him – and he knew it. The sun dipped lower, its rays painted the thunderheads with crimson as red as blood, high along their stark white towering crowns.

Still, the Mage was silent – then, he sighed, his mouth opened to speak – and he looked down.

There across his hand was Ava's blood.

A single drop of it fell; the failing light caught it, and as brilliant as a glowing drop of water it suddenly seemed – and as water, in every shade of opal, blue and green – it slowly fell, striking his boot – and impossibly spraying wide across the grass.

Like so many tears; like a thousand tears.

"You are right," he said to the Queen. "I have not the hate, nor the hunger for vengeance – but there are those who do."

He reached into his bag – and drew forth a card. He studied it, held it up – and reversed it – letting it fall – it crisped and smoked as it fell, becoming ash that lay over the grass, ash that glittered like dewdrops – like teardrops – at his feet.

I call... the West.

From the wet turf at his feet came a sound, then many – the voice of distant seas, the sweeping call of wind across limitless oceans.

First seeping, then foaming – water rose from where the blood had fallen – water clear and pure, pooling in a flood; he stepped back as, from the foaming chaos – the Undine began to rise.

Her hand reached toward him – and the Mage's wand now lay across Her iridescent palm – water ran down its length, forming into ice as it reached the air about the Elemental's hand, even as the hand rose – even as the Black Queen sought to move, strove to speak – and could not. In tones as fluid, as resonant as the echo of raindrops in ice caves – the Undine spoke – to the Dark Lady.

Thy Tears abode so long within,
From deep inside Thy heart of stone, begin
Their journey now, released. With Fire
First; now Ice shall claim Thy soul –
A frozen pyre.

357

With these my Words, my vengeance sleeps,
'Til deeper magic sows and reaps.
Hark! Feel Thou now – the UNDINE'S spell,
That binds Thee – swift and sure, and well.

Engulfed in blue flame, the Black Queen stood, motionless – and tears filled the dark eyes, tears coursed down the livid cheeks – falling as ice, turning to glittering drops of frozen light. A sheen of frozen tears lay across Her face and throat; like savage, hungry fingers, ice rose, clawing its way up and over the booted feet, across Her legs and thighs, covering the form of the Dark Lady – a form that began to change. In place of the One garbed in black and red, another figure stood – hooded and cloaked; a figure whose robes began to shimmer and smoke within the frigid prison of ice. Shifting, never constant, the form writhed; darkness opened from deep within it, it shrank, collapsing – until only eyes – blood red, glaring impotently – shone out from the darkness, finally fragmenting as flesh and blood and spirit shattered into shards of ice – dark with shadow – dark with blood.

Soon, on the grass, nothing remained of the Thing that had ruled here, cloaked in terrible majesty, reigning through terror and deceit. Lightning split the heavens – and a fine mist of rain came down, washing across the grass where the Thing had stood, cleansing it with the purity of water, of rain.

The Undine turned away; water attended Her, always underfoot, as She moved across to kneel beside the Knight. The Elemental's hand reached out – light flowed and swam like a liquid thing over the fallen warrior, as the Undine rested Her fingers over the girl's wound. The Elemental's lips moved and Her eyes closed – when they opened and She rose to Her feet, the Knight breathed a great sigh. Cass went to Ava; blood still lay on her clothes but it flowed no longer and of wound – there was none.

The Mage's wand was back at his belt. He looked up at the Elemental.

"Nay, Mage. It is not done, not yet finished; as well Thou knows. Some evil cannot be unmade, not by You, nor by Me – even as there is good that withstands all tarnishing."

Again, lightning arced overhead and the angry speech of death – thunder – and more – reached them.

"Will all now be lost?" he asked.

"Not all – there are powers here that have awakened and grown so strong, so alive – by Thy doing – and His. Seek Them; call Them and at Thy will, They will answer Thee – if Thou art strong enough, and true. Leave now if Thou canst – take Thy Knight up with Thee, but remember – Thou art Mine now, in part. In time, Thou shalt remember this – at need."

The Mage rose and stood before the Undine. They did not touch – Her form dissolved into the air as mist, all encompassing, and for one delirious moment – the Sorcerer stood cloaked, possessed, encompassed by diadems of water droplets that shimmered in all colours, and in his mind sang the voice of the sea. The mist curled away upon the wind, a wind that grew to a moaning gale.

Eyes bright, whole, and hale – the Knight was on her knees on the grass. The Mage ran to her. He pulled her to her feet— they ran, as the trees of the garden split and toppled, as the ground quaked, and the land began to fall around them.

Chapter 30

IN MEDIAS RES

"Wait!" he cried.

This time the Knight had outstripped him.

Ava halted and turned as the Mage came to her – she was close by the door of the haunted tunnel. The destruction was at their heels; trees came down behind them, and a deep chasm opened nearly at their feet.

Indomitable – for an instant – the wall held.

The Sorcerer's fists were clenched – he was not eager to shed any more of his blood. He and the Knight exchanged anxious looks. Then the Mage took a deep breath – and approached the door.

Nothing but silence met his ears this time.

The earth trembled under their feet now; great stones tumbled down from the top of the wall to land heavily before the door. Ava joined him.

"It's now – or never."

His hand rose. Fingers extended, he brought his palm directly against the scarred and ageless wood.

363

The Mage cried out – vainly, he struggled to remove his hand – a trickle of blood appeared at his nostril – and with an earth-shattering concussion, the door split right through its length and pulled off its hinges, hanging in place by a single nail.

Cass had fallen backward; on his knees in the dirt, he gasped for breath.

"It needs its pound of flesh; no matter what. Come on."

They pushed their way into the tunnel and ran forward, away from the landslide now trickling from the walls and the ceiling that fractured, threatening to come down over them. Light, dim but immeasurably welcome, began to stream down from the holes and fissures thundering into life in walls and roof.

At the tunnel's end, the door was shut. But they had reached it – Ava's kick slammed it open, and stifled with dust and ash, the two leapt through into darkness.

They landed heavily on floor – tiled floor, the floor adjoining the long corridor, lined with doors – there before them, visible and corporeal – lay the cave of twisted roots and boulders.

The elegantly worked table was beside them – it began to shake – in a moment it was dancing over a floor that rocked and shook. The table crashed over; they sprang up and raced into the cave as the floor they had left groaned and buckled and sheared.

Now they could see it – from high above, a swirl of mist and blue light.

The earth at their feet was quaking; from the walls and cave roof, stones began to pull free, tumbling down, piling up in the space.

"Go!" the Knight shouted, over the tumult of falling stone and earth.

The Mage leapt up; with root and toe hold, he pulled himself higher and higher, the Knight close behind him. He craned his neck, looking up – and cried out – now fading, becoming more and more faint was the light that had shown so brightly from above.

The gate was closing.

Earth rained down on them; tearing aside the remains of root and vine, they climbed, chasing a glow that fled away from them – hearing the voice of the vortex begin to fade. Clods of soil and stones began to choke the passage; Cass shifted his grip to a root by his head to shove them aside – and lost his footing.

For a heart-stopping second, he swung in space, with only the root to stop his plunge – he heard the vortex keening, deafening just above, and got his feet against the wall, shoving aside the dirt – when the root began to pull free.

The vortex was just above his head. He slid lower; frantically the Sorcerer reached up, up – for something, anything – his hand was still up, reaching, when the root left his grip and he began to fall.

Yet, did not – for from above, nearly out of sight in the glare of blue – another hand had taken his wrist in a grip of iron, and held him, suspended, as his boot found its place against a stone.

Amazed, Cass pulled himself higher. He looked down at Ava just below – as a large stone pulled free, tumbled past him – and struck the Knight a glancing blow across her head. Stunned, she wavered, trying and failing to keep her grip – then, inundated by a wave of stone and earth – the Knight lost her grip – and fell.

The Mage's shout was lost in the maelstrom of tortured earth and churning gate.

He was pulled up – in one instant came the wave of vertigo, of dizzying nausea –and in the next, distraught and spent, Caspian Hythe lay in a trembling heap on the cold ground at the Castle, before the altar stone.

It was not yet dawn. His breath hung in the frigid air. Garbed as he had been when he left the house in Guildford, all the breath came out of him in an agonized sob; he looked up to see Abby beside him. But he would not rise – in desperation he whirled around, looking wildly about him – back at the altar stone, with its fast-receding glow of blue light, a light that quickly disappeared, swallowed up in the dark below.

"Where is she, where is she?" he cried. "Where is Ava?"

His aunt made no answer.

The altar stone quaked.

Before his eyes, with a tremendous crash – the central stone cracked. In pieces now, it slid down, blocking the passage, barring the way to a wondrous world – an interdiction, perhaps a warning – against the way now seemingly closed.

His breath coming hard and fast, Cass sat upon the ground before the altar stone; he looked down.

In his hand was his wand.

From its surface, a thin, cold mist began to rise. For a moment, it curled like smoke about the weapon.

It hovered over his hand; in the next moment, it vanished into the wind – it was gone.

Epilogue

Equal parts of love and pity were in the eyes of Abigail Hythe as, once more – she regarded her nephew standing by the windows.

Light rain had fallen for upwards of an hour. For the greater part of that time, Cass had stood there, silently watching the rain – a look of wonder on his face.

As though he had never seen rain before – I wonder; what is he seeing now – in the rain?

Cass' wand lay beside hers on the table. She took up both and rose. She carried them to the fireplace where, upon the high mantel, a fine box had found a place. Abby placed the wands inside, marveling how – beyond all hope – the events of just the last few hours had managed, in their unfolding to allow her to see her nephew once again.

It had been still dark night only hours after the two young people had left, when it had happened.

Sitting alone in the dark, she had waited for the first, pale fingers of dawn to paint the sky – and it had come. Her wand had been in its place on the table before her. First – an uncanny silence had fallen, eating up all the life in the room. It was a silence not of peace but of expectation. Then, in the distance, the low but startling rumble of thunder; she had risen and gone to stand where Cass himself now stood. From nowhere, for the weather had been clear – bright lightning had etched the heavens and a terrible wind arose, howling across the garden, wildly scattering the leaves.

When the aunt had glanced back to the table, a light – ghostly, pale and blue, undeniably blue – had slowly gathered from no point that she could see – and settled like a sapphire mist directly over the tiger wood wand. She returned to stand over the wand, hearing words not her own, not those of anyone she could determine.

Go.

To the Castle.

Go. Seek…. And find.

Wand in hand again, she had run from the house, down the path to the Castle ruins. Then, as the first soft light of a new day had finally warmed the sky…..

The young man at the window sighed, and turned. He stopped long enough at her side to take her hand and brush his lips against it; then he climbed the stairs.

On the landing, he halted again out of habit, about to knock sadly at the locked door – and froze as though thunderstruck.

Find the Servant.

Turn the Key.

His hand went into his pocket; it came out with a small, golden key across his palm.

Time stopped when he brought the key to the keyhole of the door that could not be opened – faint whispers of voices only he could hear – then the key nestled itself into its place with a click.

The door opened; Cass stepped across the threshold.

Light came at his command although it was the switch that answered. Light filled the room – there was the desk in the corner where he had stolen his first books, there the chair that he had come to use as a youngster, after forcing his father to vacate the space with a proud laugh. For this room was

Cass' only as legacy – this room belonged to Randolph Hythe.

Now everywhere, to the son's eyes like rain to a waiting desert, came the vestiges of that life – his father's photographs, his art, his journals – all about him they lay. He looked with wonder at the photograph of his mother and the man she had chosen, seeing it clearly now, as if for the first time.

Cass exhaled; a new sensation had opened in his heart. From the chair by the desk he took up his father's sweater and smelled it – he smiled and pulled it over his own head, settling it on his tall frame, only realising then that tears were on his cheeks.

The next thing that Abby heard was the front door opening and closing. The next thing she saw was Cass as he strode around to the rear of the house, across the gardens, up the path to the Mount.

The rain had ceased.

A fresh, clean scent rose from the earth and leaves in the garden. Abby put another log on the fire, watching it glow and ignite in the flame's embrace. She touched the silver frame that held her brother's image – and she nodded.

Up on the Mount, the young man's steps halted before the grave of Lewis Carroll. To him, it was sad and grim no longer; its terrors were gone, absent were horror and fear and dread.

The fog was lowering again. He listened; no musical, rasping warble came to taunt him from among the stones. There was no call; nothing came but the teasing whisper of wind across the grass, as soft as the voice of a Sylph.

Yet should the call arise, I would not be frightened now.

There are things that do what they do, and are what they are.

What dost Thou desire?

There was no need; there was no reason, it was not a matter of life and death but the life of the spirit – a new life – that bade him say the words.

I call the East....
Of coins, the King,
From deepest earth, the wings of Spring
Traverse his caverns – GNOME arise!
The Lord of Dawn's aurora; skies
Grow bright as You appear.

From these, my hands – share power here.
Apprentice – learn!
Apprentice –wait!
I summon GNOME:
Reveal my fate.

The ground at his feet quivered; a rolling, as
of earth shifting, of rock moving – of something
waking and surfacing from fathoms deep. He stepped
back. The soil took up awful life, parting to give
form and aspect to the Elemental as it rose.

The scent of earth, of rich, life- giving earth,
moist and fertile, came up into Cass' face, even as the
Gnome appeared. His sturdy feet and limbs grew
from out of the turf itself. His hair was long,
gleaming with the sparkle of diamonds held fast
within the locks, and His face deeply bronzed, as
golden as the leaves in autumn. With eyes as bright
and deep in knowledge that only long, long years
could give, the Elemental regarded the Sorcerer who
stood before Him, and the Gnome's voice was like
the murmur of earth – labouring, ever-restless, the
deep echo of stone as it changes and spreads, giving
form and substance to the world.

The East replies...

From far below, as GNOME, I rise.
With magic deep, in vision wise.
Thy way is bound, both dark and frore.
Her form is gone, but not Her power!
Beware! What led Thee from that Land,
May turn and fail at Thy Command!
Think now as Thou dost gain this space,
What binds Thy Will? Where is Thy place?
Will Mage or Master ruler be?
Who keeps the Gate?
Who holds the Key?

The earth moved again; a spray of soil and
fine ash swept up, obscuring the Elemental – the
Gnome's form became indistinct, shadowed in mist
and ash. In a flurry of leaves, He disappeared,
leaving only the scent of earth, of loam centuries old
– and growing still. The Mage knelt; he raised a
handful of earth to his face, luxuriating in the odor
of the earth, of life itself.

What dost Thou desire?

Cass rose. He looked into the mist that seethed and furled around him – and a form appeared, drawing closer and closer to him until, finally, when the last vestiges of vapor had peeled away at last – there, just steps away – stood the Knight.

Her sword was in its sheath; her gloved hands hanging free at her side. She drew closer and halted. A warm smile lit the features of Ava Fitzalan – her eyes were still bright as the mist swelled, covering her again. Yet before she vanished, before he lost sight of her utterly, he heard her voice as it might come from a great distance.

Return.

The Knight was gone.

Caspian Hythe turned.

He walked away, finally taking the path that led to the tomb of his father; the haze began to close around the young man as he walked across the Mount.

From the tall grass near the path, with no more than a rustle – a head rose up.

Eyes, large and glittering, avidly watched the Sorcerer until the mist swallowed him up, and he was lost to view.

Only then did the Gryphon rise up from its haunches.

It turned away. Its gaze, keen and brilliant, sought the horizon. Then, with wings spread wide, as silent, and as cryptic as the mist itself – it lifted from the earth – and soared away.

END OF BOOK ONE

93399004R00228

Made in the USA
Lexington, KY
14 July 2018